# Murder at Café Miro

*The Crumbs Mysteries Book 2*

## Marilyn Boardman

Copyright © 2023 Marilyn Boardman

All rights reserved

The characters and events portrayed in this book are fictitious. Any similarity to real persons, living or dead, is coincidental and not intended by the author.

No part of this book may be reproduced, or stored in a retrieval system, or transmitted in any form or by any means, electronic, mechanical, photocopying, recording, or otherwise, without express written permission of the publisher.

ISBN: 9798851660573

Cover design by: Art Painter
Library of Congress Control Number: 2018675309
Printed in the United States of America

*Unlike my other books, where the characters are a figment of my vivid imagination, two of the characters in this book are based on real people. At their request, Al and Nariman wished to be included in the story. Café Miro opposite the University of Leeds is run by Al and Nariman in real life. My thanks to them for the gallons of tea I have consumed over the last 13 years and the chance to hide away for an hour in my unofficial office to write.*

*Follow me on Instagram @marilynboardman_novels*

# Contents

Title Page
Copyright
Dedication

| | |
|---|---:|
| Chapter One | 1 |
| Chapter Two | 4 |
| Chapter Three | 14 |
| Chapter Four | 25 |
| Chapter Five | 37 |
| Chapter Six | 47 |
| Chapter Seven | 61 |
| Chapter Eight | 69 |
| Chapter Nine | 81 |
| Chapter Ten | 88 |
| Chapter Eleven | 98 |
| Chapter Twelve | 112 |
| Chapter Thirteen | 121 |

| | |
|---|---|
| Chapter Fourteen | 133 |
| Chapter Fifteen | 145 |
| Chapter Sixteen | 156 |
| Chapter Seventeen | 173 |
| Books In This Series | 191 |
| Books By This Author | 193 |

## Chapter One

Until a few days ago looking in a mirror had never been a problem for me. Not that I am vain or a glamour puss as my Gran would have said, most definitely not. In fact, I am more likely to be checking if I have flour on my face from baking for my café, Crumbs. That or looking for new whiskers which appear overnight on my chin. Never grow old! Much as I would like to check my mascara or lipstick like other girls do, I don't have the time to apply them or see the point of it whilst baking and working so hard.

My reluctance to look in a mirror is for different reasons than anyone may think, pure fear. Being seconds away from death myself after just stumbling into a murder scene has knocked me for six. It has left me thinking hard about life.

"Come on Kitty just pick up the mirror and get it over with. You have to look sometime so make it now then I can leave you in peace," Rose said impatiently.

"Rose please don't do that, not now. I'm really not up to another confrontation." Her voice sounds so prim and proper. The same prim and proper tone my godmother had taken all through my childhood.

Two things are stopping me from looking at myself and I cannot tell her either of them. Neither have anything to do with the fact that today is my 30th birthday, certainly no fear there. You can't stop age, so my thought is to just live with it. What's another grey hair or whisker? Hair colour and tweezers were invented for those. Rose could be looking at the tear-stained divorce papers scattered across my pretty duvet cover, wrong again. Good riddance to the two-timing rat.

The truth is I am afraid to look in the mirror because it will reflect how stupid I have been. The deep red and purple line around my throat where the cord cut into my flesh as I struggled to survive will fade with time, how long will the memory of it all take? I am a total idiot trying to act like Miss Marple solving murders. At least she always survived whereas I nearly ended up wearing a name tag on my big toe in the morgue.

"Kitty, come on now I really must fly soon," Rose shouted from somewhere behind me, and there lies my second reason, my godmother Rose.

"Rose, today I am 30. Please just call me by my proper name, Kate. I am a big girl now." It has always irritated me. I hate Kitty, cats are called Kitty.

"Then act like one and look."

"You can talk. When was the last time you looked in the mirror at yourself?"

"That was very cruel my dear." Rose actually

sounded hurt.

"I'm sorry Rose, so much has happened in the last few days. I know you can't see yourself in a mirror. Ghosts don't really need to though, do they?"

"Well, it would be rather nice occasionally, especially to check my hair and my new outfits."

"Your hair was always perfect, have you changed the colour or style? If you would only show yourself again to me like the other night, then I could tell you if I like it." Well, it was worth a try.

"Kitty you know it is still grey, and no, I can't show myself to you again. I have told you I will always be there for you if you really need me, that's the best I can do. I have to fly now my dear. I'm having a meeting in Paris in half an hour and the air traffic is so bad at this time of year. I will be back soon, don't forget to have the roses and plants watered when Mr Potter comes. Oh! Just one thing, your lovely young policeman friend is on his way so do try to make yourself tidy my dear and forget the café for another day."

"How do you know he's coming Rose?" Panic rising from my hairy legs to my matted hair.

"Need you ask such silly questions, I'm going bye bye," Rose said faintly.

The room was suddenly silent.

## Chapter Two

Downstairs Crumbs, my café, sounded a lot busier than usual. The voices and laughter were drifting upstairs to my flat and through my open bathroom window from the seating in my back garden. I'm sure the recent murders, the fact they were carried out by one of our locals, and a regular customer at Crumbs had caused the extra interest. Tomorrow I will be back out front and knowing the locals of Wetherby the queues will be there. Mental note to myself to put some extra pay in my lovely staff's wages.

Without looking in the mirror I managed to get the comb through my matted hair. Putting on my long cotton dressing gown to hide my unshaved legs, well half shaved around the ankles- the bit that may be visible under my work jeggings, made me feel better. At least I look more respectable than the last time Cameron saw me, the night he helped to save me. Wearing a faded Take That T-shirt for a nightie was not a flattering look.

Murder stays in your mind long after it is all dealt with by the police. The victim and the area can be all cleared up but how do I erase from my mind all the blood, the sight of the fencing foil protruding from his stomach, walking through all that sticky blood? The memory of the cord tightening around my throat as I sat later in my own kitchen after realizing who the killer was, has left me physically and mentally scarred.

"Woof, woof."

"Come in Flossie, come on girl."

Flossie padded forward looking all around her even up at the ceiling, a favorite place for Rose to hover. Dogs can sense spirits and unlike me, my lovely Jack Russell can see Rose as well as hear her. I swear Flossie has something spiritual herself, she has a look on her face, a connection with all the spookiness around me.

"Don't worry Flossie, I'm alright. Tomorrow, I will take you for a long walk by the river. We could call in for some fish and chips for tea, how does that sound?"

"Woof," came the answer I expected, Flossie being partial to a small amount of the local fish and chips.

"OK that's a date then. After we close the café, we will go out."

Flossie seemed to grin from ear to ear at that, or maybe my painkillers have made it look like a doggy grin.

Flossie's ears have suddenly pricked up and she is standing near to the door, they're twitching.

"It's alright the policeman is coming soon, Rose told me, and you know how she knows everything." Flossie shook her head from side to side. "No, she doesn't know everything or no, Cameron isn't coming soon, which do you mean?"

Flossie keeps looking at my bedroom door and I can feel my heartbeat quickening. For a moment I actually thought it was the killer again which of course is impossible. I need to occupy my mind, get back to work. Flossie's nose is twitching from side to side like the actress in Bewitched, her ears almost turning, her radar machines at full alert.

"What's wrong girl?"

She answered by wagging her tail.

"Phew, you had me there Flossie, it's alright girl." I'd better get back to normal soon, get back my fighting spirit.

"Hello," the voice called from the stairway.

The door to my flat opened and the room is immediately engulfed in perfume. Coco Chanel to be precise. Flossie lay down and put both paws over her nose. I know the feeling, if only I could do the same! Carol breezed in looking like Elizabeth Taylor- hair, clothes, diamonds.

"How are you, my darling? I came as soon as we could get off the cruise. Let me tuck you up in bed Kate, you should be resting not walking around. Happy birthday darling your mum is here now to help you through this," Carol almost sang the words to me in her posh voice. Not the voice I recall but then nothing about her is remotely like the person I saw from time to time through my childhood.

Families can be so complicated and if we had a

choice, I'm sure many of us would change quite a few of our so called 'loved ones'. I know I would.

My big 'sister' Carol, as I was led to believe, the one I looked up to and thought was so glamorous both in looks and job on the cruise ships, was actually my mother. It was my Gran who brought me up in Headingley, Leeds with help from her best friend and next-door neighbour Rose. They were the ones always there to support me which was more than my mother ever did. It's so hard to find out the real truth when you are planning your own wedding! She did well out of working on the cruise ships and not just the travel or the good pay. Carol bagged a husband with a shed load of money to keep her happy. I do believe she loves him, and he idolises her. To be fair he is very nice to everyone he meets, quite a catch. Yes, my stepdad is a good one. He reminds me a little bit of Poirot without the Belgian accent; he has a refined Yorkshire one. His tash, as Gran would have called it, is more of a Clark Gable style than Poirot's. When you grow up with lovable oldies there's no getting away from the classic films or actors. I know most of them. Clothes and manners are definitely from the school of Poirot, but he has not the particular tottering walk. That belongs to Poirot alone.

"Now tell me what I can do for you, my birthday girl?" Carol asked whilst carefully dusting down my bedroom chair with a tissue before she parked her designer skirt and designer backside on it.

Believe me, plenty of money got spent on her figure courtesy of the Bank of Hubby. I can feel my short fuse getting shorter. Flossie whimpered in protest. She is hardly dressed to do anything to help me, and those painted talons would cut straight through my rubber gloves. Part of me, the wicked side of me, wants to ask her to clean my bathroom and loo. To see if her reshaped nose will wrinkle in surprise. No, keep calm and smile. Flossie is looking at me and her eyes seemed to be agreeing, so smile it is. OK that's enough niceness for now.

Carol handed me an envelope smiling her perfect, straight, white toothed smile. Lots of work got done on those gnashers. I remember hoping my teeth would grow straighter than my big 'sister's'. I didn't know at the time that everything was fake. Flossie put her head from side to side with a strange low growl. My word! I swear she can read my mind and she is telling me off just as my Gran would have done.

"Ok, I will behave," I said to myself.

"Woof," said Flossie which always means yes.

"Thank you," I smiled my best smile.

"Go on then, open it."

I opened the envelope to a cloud of Coco Chanel and read the over gushy verse and message written inside my pretty pink flowered card.

"It's lovely, thank you" that part was sincere, I just was not sure coming from Carol how true the gushy verse was.

"Here you are my darling, this is for you," she hugged me whilst handing me another envelope. She must dowse them in her perfume as my bedroom now smells like the Boots perfume counter, at least it has not cost me anything to smell so posh.

Something inside of me is making me feel uneasy as I hold the envelope. I felt like this before I found my murder victim. Perhaps the psychic side of me is developing, not sure I am ready for all that spooky stuff, or totally believe it.

"Go on Kitty, open it," Rose shouted from somewhere over by the window. No wonder Flossie was looking up with her whiskers twitching.

"Rose you're back, why?" I automatically said out loud.

"Sorry my darling what did you say about Rose?" Carol looked confused with one perfectly arched eyebrow up. She has never heard Rose and it's not something I can explain easily. My godmother haunts her café but don't worry she is harmless. That's a real turn off if ever I have the time to date again.

"No, I said roses are back, in the garden, pink ones, big blooms." Well, what else could I say? Pretty quick thinking for me. I'm getting good.

"You're digging a big hole my dear but carry on this is far more interesting than the meeting I had in Paris, and it was raining there." Rose sounded far too interested in my situation. She never forgave Carol for dumping me on Gran.

Reluctantly I began to open the envelope. Please do not let it be a spa day, that would be a total nightmare. All those body beautifuls filling the swimming pool and treatment rooms, ugh!

"Wow, thank you, that's something I did not expect." Flights and a stay in Madrid, three nights in a good hotel, all for me wow! How exciting. I feel quite giddy. Time to relax, breathe in all the lovely smells of Spanish food whilst walking around looking at the beautiful architecture. I know, I watch all the travel programmes.

"Carol, I think it's fantastic thank you so much." For once I actually mean it.

"I will book you into a good hotel darling and arrange the flights whenever you are ready to go. Don't you go worrying about the café after all you have been through, I am sure everyone will help. You deserve a long weekend of luxury after dealing with murderers and bodies. To think they used to sit and drink tea and have your cakes, here, in Wetherby of all places," Carol said in her over dramatic voice.

"Give me strength!" Rose shouted down from somewhere around my ceiling. "It's not before time she showed some motherly concern. Just make sure you get the best hotel; she can afford it. I will fly over now and check a few out for you my dear. Let's sting her for all we can, toodle loo, see you soon."

I presume she has flown off as it has gone quiet

again and Flossie has settled down at the side of my bed. Rose will be back soon, perhaps too soon to revel in getting back at Carol. Now why is she looking at me so intensely?

"We really must do something about your hair darling. You want to look your best with all those handsome Spaniards walking around."

"Oh no, here were go again!" I am having to control my eyeballs from rolling to the ceiling like a stroppy teenager.

"I will book you into a good salon before you go away. Some highlights in your hair will make all the difference, less mousy."

Mousy, I'm not mousy! Carol does have a point about needing my hair styled. It's a little longer than usual and bed tousled but I resent her telling me what to do. I am what I call a 'combaphobic' and proud of it. That means a quick comb through on a morning and that's it. Look at her, she's practically stripping me from my head to my toes and it's not a nice feeling. Good job she hasn't looked in my underwear drawer, big is best. I go for comfort not style, bring on the Bridget Jones's look. I once tried thongs, well twice actually, for my rat of a husband, isn't it usually for men? As I walked, I felt like a magician's assistant being sawn in two, my rear area.

"Don't worry about booking for me Carol, I am quite happy going to my usual hairdresser." I am trying to sound strong, honestly.

"Really? Oh well darling, we can discuss it

nearer the time."

Considering my lifestyle which is wake up, bake up and dash from table to table serving or in the kitchen, why do I need fancy hairstyles? My trips out on an evening are to walk Flossie and to go to the wholesalers. I really do not have the energy at the end of a long day in Crumbs to shave my legs and doll myself up just for that. Wow, legs, I will have to do them for Madrid unless Spaniards find hairy legs attractive, not many men do. Having a single life does have its advantages one of which is a quick run around the ankles with my shaver. When trousers or leggings are the normal dress code that is enough, nothing gets seen higher than that. Oh oh, here we go! Carol keeps looking at her expensive Rolex wristwatch and frowning. I thought it was all too good to be true.

"Is something wrong Carol?"

"Nothing darling. I just hoped to have more time with you before leaving."

"Where are you going? You only came back today."

"New York darling, it's a business trip. I'm just going along to support Lawrence and make sure he doesn't get up to any mischief on an evening. We do have a few invitations to dinner and a garden party to attend but apart from that it will be quite boring for me."

Boring. How can Carol say it will be boring? She will have his platinum credit card burning away in her purse as she shops 'til she drops. I suppose I should consider myself lucky to have seen her for a full 45 minutes.

"Now darling, promise me you will have a long soak in the bath and then get dressed, it will make you feel so much better. Oh, and don't forget to lock the doors." Carol is fussing and blowing kisses as she walks towards the bedroom door which normally, I would feel is over the top but strangely, I don't today. Cringeworthy.

"Promise me darling."

"I promise Carol. Go on before you miss your flight."

Flossie is looking at me with one ear up and one down, her head to the side. If she could speak Human, I know what she would say.

"I know Flossie, but she means well. I think I will have the bath and perhaps go downstairs and see what's going on in the café before Cameron arrives. You stay here and let me know if anyone comes upstairs."

"Woof."

## Chapter Three

There is something magical about soaking up to your neck in bubbles. All your aches, pains, cares and worries can be sorted out whilst semi floating in the luscious froth. This and baking are when I am able to think clearly, almost see through the mist that everyday life brings and sort it all out. Well nearly all.

"Hello, my dear, I'm back from sunny Spain," Rose's voice blasted through the flowery scented steam, from somewhere over the toilet area this time.

"Strewth Rose, don't do that! You could have drowned me with the shock, and it would be nice if you could let me have some privacy, please."

"Kitty, I saw it all when you were little, don't be such a prude."

It's pointless arguing with her as this is a conversation we have had several times before. At least this time I wasn't on the toilet with my knickers around my ankles!

"Did you enjoy your flying trip?"

"Well, it is very difficult to enjoy such a short visit my dear, especially at the speed we travel. Still, I did get a chance to cause a bit of a fuss in a few places," Rose chuckled.

"Rose, how could you?"

"Quite easily my dear. Young people these days have no morals. Hopping in and out of bed with their secretaries and pretending to be married."

"It's been going on since Adam and Eve, don't tell me you didn't know that, Rose. Sex was invented a long time ago by them. It took too many centuries to invent television and show more films. Whilst we are on the subject, please can I ask you more about Carol?" My water is going to turn me into a prune if I don't get out of the bath soon, but this is something that's been bothering me since my recent near-death experience.

"What on earth would you want to ask about her my dear? Your Gran told you all she wanted to let you know."

"Everything except who my father is." There, I have said it!

"That's because we never knew, and she would never tell us. Carol was always what we called a bit flighty, a 'fast cat' your Gran would say. Boys were always hanging around the corner waiting for her to put on her lipstick. She looked older than her years and it was very difficult for your Gran to control her. With no mobile phones in those days, she had no idea where Carol was or who she was with. It was like a time bomb waiting to go off from her thirteenth birthday. Not a good time, lots of screaming and temper tantrums." Rose sounds quite upset remembering the past so perhaps it's time to pull the plug, in all ways.

With the information Rose has given me on hotels in Madrid I should be able to find somewhere really nice to book into. A night on the computer with cake and coffee sounds ideal. Flossie needs to go behind the shed to do her usual. At least she has privacy unless that hedgehog comes out and about early.

"Come on Flossie, let's go downstairs and find out some gossip. Don't look at me like that, you know you love it too."

"Woof."

Downstairs most of the tables inside Crumbs are occupied and several outside on the patio also. A noticeable hush in the conversations as soon as I appeared made me feel uncomfortable.

"How lovely to see you up and about and downstairs Kate." Mr Potter, a true gentleman, customer, part time staff member plus my gardener and dogwalker to Flossie, is giving me a hug. I don't know what I would do without him.

"Thank you, it's good to see you all again. I will just get a coffee and you can tell me what I have missed, please join me."

By the time all the well-wishers had greeted me, most of them really wanting the gory details first-hand of the near fatal evening (which I am not supplying them with) more than coffee is needed.

Sally my wonderful assistant, friend and cousin of the handsome detective Cameron, is gliding through the tables and coming to my rescue.

"Why don't you go into the garden with Mr Potter, and I will bring tea, coffee and cake for you both. Smell the lavender, that will perk you up Kate," Sally winked as she steered me away from another table of locals straining their necks to look at my bruises.

"Good idea Sally, thank you for being so kind." Mental note to myself to make sure they both get something extra in their pay packets this week.

Sally works hard, runs a home and has three children to look after. She is gold hearted; I am very lucky to have her. I am lucky to have my staff and friends who had helped over the last few days.

"Mr Potter the pink roses are starting to look better now you have fed them, thank you. I know Rose will love them."

"Will?" Mr Potter is looking strangely at me.

"I mean would have loved to see them blooming so well. They were what she planted down the path when she first bought Crumbs." Wow, I need to be more careful as nobody else has the 'pleasure' of Rose's return visits, only me. Poor thing, he may be thinking I am suffering from the trauma of the deaths and the Wetherby psychos who caused them.

"Let's take a table near to them and away from the orange geraniums if you don't mind." I suddenly feel a little queasy after looking at the bright orange.

"Shall I move the pots, Kate? I apologise I did not think about them."

"No, honestly I am alright please leave them where they are. It was just a quick recollection that's all, it has passed."

It was as I looked at them the other night that I had my Miss Marple moment, and I knew who the murderer was, and she also knew and then came after me.

"Here we are, coffee for you Kate and tea for Mr Potter. This cake is delicious Kate, but I am afraid there is only one left in the freezer. Plenty of other cakes though and two large bags of scones. It's a good job you bake so much, murder has made the curious locals extremely hungry. What a boost for business but please promise us you will not repeat it, ever!" Sally looks really tired, and I feel so guilty for putting extra pressure on her.

"It's not something I ever want to repeat Sally. Baking and the café are more than enough excitement for me." Boy do I mean that!

"Thank you, don't worry I will be back in tomorrow bossing you all around. Perhaps you can take the afternoon off tomorrow to relax before your husband comes around shouting at me."

Sally looked at me with one eyebrow up, a look I know so well when she is dealing with a difficult customer.

"As if he would ever dare to. He has his moments, but he knows what this job means to me. The extra money helps us so much I don't think he would want me to leave. At least it has taught him how to turn the washing machine on, and he can hang out washing now. Sometimes upside down but it still dries. He is so domesticated now his mother hardly recognises him." Sally chuckled and winked again.

It's good to see the garden and sit with such lovely people. Even though I made the cake myself I have to say it's really good. Flossie has been behind the shed to have her tiddle and now seems busy watching a bee. With her head going from one side to the other her ears moving and her tail wagging, I'm sure she is talking to it. Flossie has some rare qualities, but nobody would ever believe me if I told them.

My own ears are beginning to zoom in on an interesting conversation coming from the table to my immediate left. Let's face it, all cafés are full of interesting characters and of course lots of gossip. Two of my regular ladies, both from Wetherby, are very knowledgeable about the goings on of many of the locals, prominent and otherwise. They are always the first to know everything, but of course never want to 'gossip' about anyone. How they find it all out I will never know, but they always manage to. These ladies certainly have their antennae tuned in, day and night.

Miss Hall and Miss Winters are firm friends who worked together in the local library for years. As both are now retired, they continue to meet two or three times a week at Crumbs to discuss matters of 'interest'. To the rest of us it's pure gossip but it can be interesting. It's always struck me how much alike they look from height, grey curly hair and round gold framed glasses sitting on short noses to their well-spoken voices.

"No, he never married although he was quite a catch in his day, too young for us Peggy, more's the pity." Miss Hall giggled in a girlish way.

"Sounds like he is making up for lost time now Jean," Miss Winters laughed as she wiped chocolate buttercream from the corner of her mouth. "I heard he has several women on the go coming on different nights of the week. Mostly Monday to Saturday, Sunday being a day of rest!"

"You can never tell Peggy, he used to be so quiet in the library. I could rarely get a sentence out of him when he brought books to the desk. He had a strange choice of books as I recall." Miss Hall paused with her fork in mid-air loaded with strawberry gateau and cream. Slowly it began to fall off into a creamy, mushy heap on her plate.

"Careful Jean, that's your new blouse." Miss Winters quickly pushed a couple of paper serviettes towards her friend. "What kind of books? Nothing too racy, I hope. All that sex and disgusting slushy stuff, terrible."

"Well not from our library but who knows what he got in Leeds or Harrogate. I remember asking him if he was taking a course or something as all the books were to do with fashion, ladies fashion."

"How very strange, Jean. Especially as he is not a very well-turned-out gentleman. I know he has to wear a boiler suit to take care of all the jobs at the

Town Hall, but he doesn't really smarten himself up outside of work either." Peggy Winters is all ears at the new information.

Ah! That description fits another of my customers, one I am sure Mr Potter will know more about. I only know him as a customer, a very quiet one and polite too.

"Mr Potter, do you know the caretaker at the Town Hall at all?"

"You are talking about Mr Greaves, Kate?" Mr Potter hardly ever takes part in the local ladies' gossip. I suppose he knew first-hand what it was like as his own marriage had been a difficult one. Until his wife's death he had been at her beck and call with next to no thanks or kind words from her. Now his life has begun again. Helping me, going to society meetings and best of all meeting up again with his first true love. The local gossips will be loving it all.

"The quiet gentleman who always sits in the corner, a toasted teacake and tea for one." I may be surprised one day if he orders something totally different.

"That's the one. I know he has worked at the Town Hall for a few years now. He seems to keep himself to himself. Not a loner by any means as he is very pleasant if you can ever get into conversation with him."

"I see. Have you ever actually had a proper conversation with him?"

"Kate, what is going on, why are you fishing?

What do you need to know about him?"

"Nothing really, just interested in my customers, that's all..." Well, I don't want Mr Potter thinking badly of me.

"Oh, I know that look, Kate, so what is going on?" Mr Potter repeated.

After telling him quietly as the ladies were still at their table next to us, Mr Potter didn't answer. He seemed to be thinking it all through, so I poured him some more Earl Grey tea and sat back waiting.

Mr Potter looked me in the eyes and said in a hushed voice "I don't think there is anything untoward going on Kate. He is a decent man, does a good job for the Town Hall and keeps a very tidy garden."

Just because he keeps a tidy garden does not mean he is so perfect. Maybe I am too suspicious, people are good at lying and hiding things. My life with Matt the big Rat was based on lies and deceit. I bet the Yorkshire Ripper was out there mowing his lawn on a Sunday and planting his marigolds. There we are, I once read somewhere that in Victorian flower language marigolds are for malice, exactly my point.

"Well, my Gran would have said there is no smoke without fire so let us see what else our two Wetherby lady detectives find out. I am quite sure one of us will overhear something at their next coffee meet up."

"Really Kate, I don't sit with my tea listening to customers' conversations. If I hear anything it usually goes in one ear and out of the other. Flossie is the one to hear more but she can't tell you," he said with a smile.

Sad but true. Flossie would have made a good undercover agent for me but that has given me an idea-Rose. I am sure she will enjoy floating around, picking up snippets of information. I just have a feeling there is something going on even though I don't want to get involved. Call it intuition, a feeling in my waters, there is a mystery developing, indeed there is.

Mr Potter is putting all his crockery neatly onto the tray. I tell him not to, but he is such a lovely person, always ready to help others. Today I am saying nothing. It's so nice to just sit and be helped that I am soaking up the fussing and enjoying it whilst I can.

"Come on Flossie, shall we have a walk by the river?" Mr Potter is calling to Flossie who is sprawled in the shade down at the bottom of the garden near the gate.

"Woof."

Flossie would never turn down a walk especially with Mr Potter who sneaks her treats. Everyone does, the ice cream man, the fish and chip shop but it doesn't seem to be harming her. I wish I could stay as slim as her.

"Be a good girl Flossie and don't chase the ducks."

Flossie looked at me for a moment before shaking her head from side to side with the answer of 'no'. A little too hesitant for my liking but that's Flossie all over, her intentions are good, but she likes the chase.

"Have fun, I will see you later my lovely girl."

"Woof."

## Chapter Four

"Hello Kate, how are you?"

"Gosh! You made me jump Cameron, I was just closing my eyes and relaxing." Whilst trying to listen a bit more to Miss Hall and Miss Winters of course. Shame, nothing interesting was discussed and thankfully they are now leaving so they cannot overhear my conversation with the dishy detective.

"Can I get you a drink and something to eat?"

Gosh his eyes are gorgeous!

"Sally has got my order, thank you."

Ooh that smile should come with a health warning!

"Do you need me for anything? Although I don't think I can tell you more than I did." If my heart flips again he will think I am going to faint. Again.

"No, nothing else will be needed until the case goes to court. I just wanted to make sure you are alright and resting well," Cameron said full of concern.

"I am fine, honestly. Lots happening all at once, but I can cope. Today I am alive, a year older and a single woman again with a weekend in Madrid to look forward to."

"That is a lot in one go and I like the single status."

Whoosh, my temperature has just risen to 110! My cheeks are on fire, how old am I, 13 or 30? Breathe girl. Calm down. This is a handsome man who saw you in your old Take That T-shirt as a nightie, hairy legs on display and a piece of cord around your neck making your mascaraless eyes pop. If after all that he can still sit opposite me, looking drop dead gorgeous and wanting to be with me then, WOW!

Cameron stayed long enough to eat, drink and send my heart into a spin before a phone call pulled him back to work and me to reality. I think I will cool down by looking at the surplus stock in the freezer. Tomorrow needs to be back to normal so baking will be my early morning task followed by another busy day serving and smiling my way through the tables. In a café two days are never the same, that's why I love it so much.

"Come on Kate back to your flat to rest. If you intend to be back tomorrow, take advantage of doing nothing except watching films and then an early night," Sally said gently.

"I think I will. Thank you, Sally, pop up before you leave."

"Will do."

Skimming through the films they all seem to be murder or spies so a crime film it is. Well, what can I say other than I am a sucker for a good mystery.

It's a beautiful morning with blue skies and a big sun shining down. Flossie and I have been out early to the river for a walk and now the kitchen surfaces are full of baking utensils, ingredients and cooling racks in place, ready to be stacked when the oven timer goes off. Flossie's whiskers are really twitching and judging by her nose she is pleased to have all the wonderful sweet, chocolatey and fruity smells whizzing through the air. Even with my kitchen door open and the extractor fan on full it's heavenly. Flossie also knows she will get a few little corners broken off (as I will-baker's privilege) when everything is cool, and I am ready to decorate the cakes.

"Right Flossie I have to close the door whilst I have a shower so are you in or out?" That's exactly what my Gran used to say when I was little and wanted to play in the garden but kept running back into the house. It drove her bonkers especially when my friends followed me. Such happy childhood days, thanks Gran, thanks Rose.

"Hello, my dear did you call me?" Rose piped up from behind me.

"No Rose, I was just remembering happy childhood days with you and Gran. What are you up to today?" How stupid I feel talking to my ceiling, people would think I am mad if they witnessed it.

"A few of us are meeting up in Monaco soon

to have some fun in the casino," Rose chuckled. When Rose chuckles it's always a bad sign.

"Rose! I don't like the sound of that. Your idea of fun will be blowing the ball on the roulette table, turning over the dice someone has thrown and altering the scores on those one-armed bandit machines."

"As I said my dear, fun. Anyway, don't forget to book your hotel for Madrid. Must dash the air traffic will be getting clogged and I have to be there in time for cocktails."

There is no point in talking about that either. Even I know ghosts cannot eat or drink, at least I didn't think they could, and it seems early for cocktails.

"Rose, before you go, I want to tell you something I overheard. If at some point you can check if it is correct or you hear anything else, you can let me know."

"No time to stop and listen now Kitty, so transfer your thoughts through to me as I fly. It will be like all that inflight entertainment on the planes."

"How?" This is all so new to me. I don't think there is a manual on how to communicate with resident ghosts. Page 15, transferring thoughts to deceased godmother as she flies to do mischief.

"Kitty, just stand in the shower, close your eyes if you have to and say it all in your head. Both of us will be multitasking then, no time wasted. Toodle pip my dear."

"Rose, don't go yet I need to ask you more about it."

No answer, too late she has flown!

I am not sure if being covered in Dove soap will have interfered with any of the wavelengths or not but at least I have tried. There is a first for everything and boy is this a first. As Rose has not replied yet in any shape or form, I suppose I will have to wait until the next surprise visit.

The blinds are up, the door sign is on "Welcome we are open" and I am ready and waiting for the first customers of the morning to arrive. Music, that's what I forgot, perhaps something smooth like Michael Bublé. Now I feel so much better, even Flossie has her tail swaying in time with his velvety tones.

"Morning Kate, it's a beauty, isn't it?" Sally sang along with Michael as she hung her jacket behind the kitchen door. "I've brought you some raspberries, strawberries and blueberries. Oh, and before I forget, George at the fruit shop sends his love." Sally busied herself putting the fruit in the fridge and then checked the tables were all clean and everything ready for customers to enjoy.

Teapots of different sizes and patterns are sparkling on the long shelf in the kitchen. A smaller shelf above them has only three very special teapots. These belonged to Gran and Rose, and I never use them for my customers. Trays are already lined with a pretty scalloped paper tray cover. Cups, saucers, and plates in an array of pretty colours and patterns are clean and stored on another shelf. Charity shops and car boot sales provide me with most of my china. Each time I go to buy crockery, even though I try really hard, I cannot resist anything with pretty flowers on it. They are so delicate, and so pretty and feminine. I have bought sets with men in mind, although nobody has ever complained about drinking from a flowery cup. Still one thing I will not have in my shop is a beaker/mug. Taking tea or coffee and cake should be an occasion to take pleasure in, not rushed or huddled with hands warming around the beaker/mug.

"Next time you are buying stock Kate, we could do with some more cake forks and teaspoons. They seem to walk out of the door along with some customers. I am getting to the point when if I see a lady with an overly large handbag, I watch the teapots and cake stands."

"Human nature I'm afraid Sally. That's why prices get put up in all the shops to cover those light-fingered selfish people who cannot stop themselves from stealing. Would you believe that some of the pinchers actually think because they bought a tea and piece of cake, they have bought the fork or teaspoon. One customer actually said that to me when I worked here for Rose."

"Cheeky devil!" Sally said. "Who was it? Does she still come in here because my eyes will be boring into her back the whole time she is here."

"No, not anymore because I added them all onto

her bill and she was too embarrassed when I said loudly what the extra charge was for."

"Good for you, I will remember that one." Sally moved forward to greet Crumbs' first customer of the day, our friend, merry widow and hotel owner Pippa Davenport.

"Good morning, ladies. How are you, Kate?" Pippa asked.

"I'm fine thanks, trying to get everything back to normal, that's the only way I can deal with it."

"Well, I think you are very brave Kate. Come here and let me give you a big hug." Pippa held her arms out wide.

Pippa is a lovely lady, very classy and she could certainly give Carol a few lessons in sincerity. For all her loveliness I always feel life has not been too kind to her. Two dead husbands, a string of suitors but nobody she could trust not to be after her nice bank balance. Both husbands left her a considerable amount of money on their deaths and the last husband left her the Davenport Manor Hotel.

Davenport Manor had been the family's home for a few hundred years. Set in acres of beautiful countryside ideal for horse riding (her second husband met his demise galloping around the estate), shooting parties, weddings and her brand-new venture of spa days and wild water swimming. With a small lake in the grounds, on-trend wild water swimming had to be the next attraction. Personally, I could not stand fish swimming around my body. I really would panic if they touched me. Panic to the point of arms thrashing around, near fainting and needing rescuing from drowning. That will not be on my wish list. I have never forgotten the squirming sensation of a shrimp that found its way into my bikini bottoms whilst swimming in the sea with the Rat on our honeymoon in Bournemouth. My goodness it was disgusting! Not Bournemouth, I love all around that end of our country. No, the pervy shrimp in my bikini bottoms was awful! So was he, Matt the Rat, but that sensation is slowly passing.

As Pippa broke free from me, I sensed she had not come just to see how I am, although that part will be genuine. Immaculately dressed as usual, even when casual, in cream trousers, a black floaty top and a cream, black and tan silk scarf draped over one shoulder. Even the gold chain of her gorgeous black designer handbag stays over her shoulder. I have to put mine across my chest or it drops off all the time. Wrong shoulder shape perhaps, anyway something is on her mind. I can tell by her eyes and the pinched look around them. Pippa usually glows and her eyes are normally large and sparkly, making people feel her warmth and friendliness.

"Have you got time for a tea or a coffee, Pippa?" I need to sit her down and see if she will open up to me.

Pippa looked at her dainty gold watch, frowned,

then smiled showing her pearly white teeth. Lots of dental work done there but I have to say for her age, well worth every penny she spent on them. Note to self - dentist appointment, no more putting it off.

"Have you got any of your delicious cinnamon toast to go with it please?"

Sally jumped in. "Of course, Pippa. How many slices would you like?"

"I should say one slice, but I think I need two if you can and tea, please." Pippa said sitting down with an unusually deep sigh.

"I'll just get some coffee to kick start myself. Then I will have a rest and a chat with you."

As I walked into the kitchen to the lovely wafts of cinnamon, Sally gave me a knowing look.

"Nearly ready, go and sit back down with Pippa. I have your coffee cup ready; do you want anything to eat Kate?" Sally had her mothering look on her face.

"No thanks I had some cereal earlier and it's going to be hard not to nibble my way through the day."

The truth is I tried on a few skirts and dresses I haven't had out of the wardrobe in a long time, that's when it hit me, weight gain. Lots of weight gain! If I put off Madrid for another month and live on lettuce leaves then I should be back on track, if I don't side track. That's a lot of ifs so no promises there. I swear just by baking daily and breathing in all that sweetness the weight goes on without it even tickling the inside of my mouth.

Pippa was anxiously scrolling through her messages on her iPhone. She must be anxious as she's biting down hard on her perfectly coral lip glossed bottom lip.

"Here we are Pippa, two cinnamon toasts with extra cinnamon and tea and coffee for you Kate, enjoy," Sally said with a smile.

"Thank you, Sally." Pippa returned the smile.

"Thank you, I will come back when I have drunk this," I said giving her a knowing look.

I thought I would let Pippa enjoy at least one slice whilst it was still hot. The wait is making me more curious. Suddenly I realised that Pippa's eyes had filled up with tears, she was still nibbling her way through her last slice. Do I stop her or let her finish? Who am I to stop her eating although tears are now dropping onto her plate? That's it, I'm in there.

"Pippa, what on earth is wrong? Is the toast that bad?" Well, I am only trying to lighten the atmosphere. Pippa made a little choking noise, perhaps I've made it worse.

"Oh dear, I am so sorry Kate. I should not have come, it's unfair to you but I just had to get away from the hotel. Crumbs felt safe and so comforting and ... oh dear." Pippa dabbed her thankfully waterproof mascaraed eyes.

I held her other hand and hoped she would tell me more.

"Is there a problem with the hotel? You always

seem to be fully booked."

"No, not the hotel. I thought my life was just getting back on track, my personal life I mean, then things started happening."

Oh, so it is another Rat who has broken her heart again, I thought so. Pippa looked at me as though she had just read my mind.

"No, it's not man trouble, and Antonio is wonderful, so attentive and a true gentleman."

Really! I have seen him once in Wetherby with Pippa at the bank, something made me want to step away from him. Perhaps I just don't like men anymore, well except for one, if I get the chance.

"What is it then? You are not the type to give in and cry." That is so true, knowing her and what she has gone through in the last year.

"Someone is sending horrible messages to me, day and night for the last few weeks."

"Can you tell me what they are about? I mean only if you want to of course. Don't tell me anything too personal."

Pippa looked all around her, but the only other customer was further away in a corner and Mrs Clegg is stone deaf, bless her. We would hear if she had turned up her hearing aid because it makes a terrible screeching noise.

"They are always warning me, telling me not to part with any money, not to be taken in by his charms." Pippa looked distressed. I knew it! They have to mean Antonio, all very handsome dark hair (possibly dyed as at his age it has to be). A smooth-talking Spaniard. I can tell them a mile off. I must ask Rose when she next floats in.

"Have you been careful Pippa? I know it's difficult and it's your life but whoever it is must have their reasons for warning you."

"I don't have to pay for anything when he takes me out, he is fun and charming. It can't be Antonio they are messaging me about because he is good and very loving." Pippa said with her blusher turning a shade deeper.

"Have you shown the messages to anyone at the police station? They will advise you what to do."

"No, you are the first to know Kate. I feel too embarrassed to show them."

"Don't worry I can have a word with the nice detective who is helping me. He may want to look at your phone so can I ask him to call on you at the hotel, keep it more private that way?"

"Thank you, Kate, that would be better. Please ask him to ring me when he wants to come, I'm there every afternoon." Pippa looked a little easier already, unlike me.

# Chapter Five

During my short lunch break in the garden, I managed to contact Cameron and explain Pippa's situation. Part of me felt guilty as it was also a good excuse to hear his voice again. Cameron is ringing her to arrange a visit this afternoon so I hope she can get some reassurance from him. It's strange but I can't get rid of the creepy feeling I had when I saw Antonio with Pippa. Something bothered me then and is bothering me even more now.

We must have served gallons of tea and coffee today to thirsty inquisitive customers. My cake sales are double the usual sales for one day, all good for the bank balance. As an old friend who runs Miro, a café in Leeds, always says "business is business". Murder brings the rubbernecks out so let's be pleasant and treat them as we always treat our customers, smile, be courteous and be in control. As soon as I can I need to make a list of ingredients to buy. If this continues, I will be baking all through the night to get plenty of spare cakes in the freezer, this is when I wish my Gran could help me. Gran taught me to bake, she was the best.

Miss Hall and Miss Winters have just arrived,

where is Rose when I need her? Should I try transferring thoughts again? I don't even know if she got the last ones, but it's worth a try. Here goes. "Rose if you are free, please can you pop in? Oh, my word I can't say 'for a coffee' can I so please just pop in." Right, I've tried, I'll keep my eyes open the best I can in between serving and clearing the tables.

So far, they seemed to have talked about most of the inhabitants of Wetherby except Mr Greaves and I desperately need to go to the loo. My bladder feels the size of a balloon and it could explode very soon. A wink in Sally's direction is our mutual message so I'm now feeling much better in my own loo upstairs, boss's privilege. Looking down at my half-mast pants and hairy legs have put another note to self in action, new underwear needed!

"You certainly could do with some my dear," Rose piped up. "If not, you will need to carry a safety pin in your purse in case the elastic goes."

"ROSE! You have done it again, why do you do it at such awkward moments?"

Rose tutted somewhere in front of me. "It's not my fault you call me at the wrong times, is it? I came when I could, now don't argue my dear just tell me what you want me to do." Rose's voice has taken on her prim tone again.

Button it Kate if you need her to help you, my inner voice is telling me.

"Quite right my dear."

My mouth is open to say something but it's pointless. "So, you have got my thoughts transferred Rose, that's good I don't have to repeat myself. Anything to report back from either Mr Greaves or the ladies downstairs?"

"Mr Greaves had a lady visitor leave around 9:30 PM. A very stylish lady in fact I recognised the blue outfit she was wearing. The heels should have been a little higher for the length of her skirt but who knows what she is comfortable wearing. Nicely styled chestnut brown hair in a short bob and a handbag not a shoulder bag, good quality black leather. Ladies so seldom carry a smart handbag these days, always shoulder bags."

"And did Mr Greaves come to the doorstep to say goodbye?"

"No, he was not at the door at all," Rose said. "Come to think of it he didn't even call out to her or she to him."

"That is strange, well done." My mind is racing with all the reasons for him not being in the doorway. "Any chance of you going inside his house Rose?"

"Not a chance! It's against the Ghost's code of practise to spy that much unless someone is in danger, or we are sent by our superiors."

"But you do it to me Rose, look, now." How come ghosts go into houses and scare the living daylights out of people? It doesn't make sense to me but then none of my situation with Rose makes sense.

"You are family Kate, and against my advice my dear you are making a habit of putting yourself in danger."

"Okay, thanks, if you do over here or see any more, please just let me know. Something is feeling strange about all this and when I get my niggly feelings it's like an itch that won't go without a good scratch. I have to go Rose before Sally thinks I have a problem; poor thing has worried enough about me the last few days. Fly safely, be good."

"I'm always good my dear, just having fun. Take care my dear."

Rose seemed to have flown and so must I, downstairs.

Thirty rock buns, one cherry loaf cake, one Madeira cake, two coconut loaves and a fruity farmhouse cake later, all cooling on racks and now I'm jiggered. It's 9 PM. Have I eaten? Not sure, but I really can't be bothered.

"Flossie, Flossie girl come on let's have a walk."

I can have the rest of the chicken and some salad when I get back, or fish and chips by the river. Flossie enjoyed her bits of chicken with her dried food earlier followed by corners of cake for a treat.

Flossie is padding towards me with her lead in her mouth and her tail sweeping the floor of the kitchen.

"Ready?"

"Woof."


Apart from a few noisy teenagers hanging around the bandstand down by the river, it's fairly quiet. My normal evening walk always takes me along the river to a few streets away from Mr Greaves' cottage so why not? I'm only going to walk past, nothing wrong with that, but if I see anything interesting that will be good.

Mr Greaves lives in the middle of a row of cottages, all very neat and tidy, with well-kept gardens. They were the original cottages but are now surrounded by large blocks of stone fronted modern flats going for ridiculous prices, bought and then rented out for ever more ridiculous prices. The front block looks out over the river Wharfe, pretty but to me too noisy because of the constant roar of the water. It also reminds me of my life married to Matt the Rat. We lived near the water's edge in a flat by the Royal Armouries in Leeds, not all pleasant memories. Mr Greaves' cottage has a beautiful pink climbing rose around the shiny dark blue doors with a shiny brass door knocker and letterbox. He keeps it well polished. If I stay on the opposite side of the road, I will have a good view walking up slowly to the end of the row of cottages. I can always use Flossie as an excuse to stop for a while.

A quick glance at my watch is showing it's approaching 9:28 PM, the bewitching time. Oh my! Bingo! The blue door is opening. I can see the back of a lady with short curly blonde hair. Why is she coming down the two steps to the front doors backwards? That's odd, she's pulling the door hard to close it, lifting the handle upwards and putting it into a locking position then checking the door. If Mr Greaves was the other side of the door, I'd expect him to be doing all the locking. I hope he is not ill in bed and I'm here thinking the worst of the poor man.

The lady visitor is wearing a burgundy trouser suit with cream flat shoes, a cream shoulder bag and a cream, burgundy and pink scarf. Very smart, it looks like a linen suit as there are a couple of creases behind the knees from sitting for a while inside the cottage.

"Come on Flossie, I need you to stall a little opposite the next cottage. Can you do that girl?"

"Woof."

Good as her woof Flossie has stopped to sniff around a gate post. Certainly psychic my dog. Perhaps Rose can tell me more about Flossie's powers. It will be wonderful if she is.

"That's it Flossie have a good sniff, take your time girl. I need a good look at this lady."

"Woof."

The lady in burgundy is medium height and medium build, nothing outstanding there. Hair curled but looks natural, not a tight perm curl as Rose used to have. I can only see a little of her face side on and she is now walking down the street with her head slightly bent so it's not so easy to see much of her features. One thing I have noticed is how she puts her right leg forward, as though the knee will click when weight is put on it. Yes, that's how it looks. Poor thing she may have an injury and has to wear flats to walk in for comfort. The movement is not as fluid as with her left leg. On the corner of the street a taxi is waiting, and Mr Greaves' lady friend quickly gets into the back, and they are driving off on the road to Leeds. Is it me thinking too much but why not order a taxi to the cottage?

"What do you think Flossie, odd behaviour or not?"

"Woof," Flossie agreed.

"Right girl time for home, some salad and an early night, we'll do fish and chips another night."

"Woof."


It's absolutely pouring down with rain this morning so I'm not expecting a rush of customers unless they are out shopping and want to dry out. Our door is always open for soggy customers and to let the steam out! Rose drilled it into me to keep fresh air flowing through. Even in winter when we have to switch some heating on, the small top windows are pushed open.

"Good morning, ladies. Can I take your umbrellas from you and put them in the umbrella stand?" That way the floor stays dry.

"Thank you, Kate, that is kind of you it's such a dreadful morning. We didn't want to stay at home all day with nothing but daytime television to watch, so here we are," Miss Hall smiled happily.

"You are very welcome, tea for two and toasted

fruited tea cakes for you both?"

"Yes please," they said in unison.

Sally was just putting on her apron and smiled a knowing smile from the bottom end of the counter.

Miss Hall and Miss Winters both bought one of the new stone-built apartments on their retirement. My information from Sally, who seems to know everyone in Wetherby is that Miss Winters lives at the front overlooking the river and Miss Hall at the back overlooking the cottages. Interesting indeed, I bet a lot of curtain twitching goes on in Miss Hall's apartment. With a bit of luck, they might continue their usual 'hot news reports' on the residents of Wetherby, especially on Mr Greaves.

Sally brought over tea and hot buttered fruited tea cakes fresh from the toaster.

"Thank you Sally they smell delicious," Miss Winters said, tucking her paper napkin down the neck of her pale blue jumper to save any butter drips from staining.

"Enjoy them ladies, let me know if you want any more tea or hot water."

"We will, thank you," they said together.

"I saw her last night Peggy," Miss Hall said excitedly.

"Saw who Jean?" Miss Winters said trying not to lose a sultana from her mouth.

"Why Mr Greaves' lady friend of course Peggy. I was just closing my curtains, looked across the road and there she was as bold as brass leaving the cottage and walking down the street to a taxi. Down the street mind you, not outside his gate like anybody who was not worried of being seen."

"Well I never!" Miss Winters said, clearly thrilled at the news. "Was it the one you heard about, the one with red hair?"

"No, a brassy blonde no less, obviously bleached."

"Mmm." Miss Winters had just taken another bite and was not going to waste any of it.

"Anything else to do with the Spaniard that Pippa Davenport is all cow eyed over? You would think at her age she would know better Jean. Never trust a man who won't let go of your hand after shaking it, Jean. Mark my words he is as slimy as a toad."

Miss Winters has the measure of Antonio Lopez alright, slimy as a toad what a good description. I think I will clean a few tables nearby so I can keep it working.

"He was in the post office queue yesterday and the atmosphere seemed to totally change," Miss Hall said thoughtfully.

"In what way?"

"Well, people seemed on edge, yes that's it, on edge. Susan Walsh was serving Mr Greaves some stamps and then when she looked up and saw him behind in the queue she tensed. Her face looked like thunder and she wasn't friendly towards him, in fact for her, she was quite rude. Then Mr Greaves turned, saw him and rushed out without saying hello to me. He usually nods and says hello at least."

I can't keep cleaning the tables or they will know I'm listening but what I have heard has been enlightening. A phone call to Pippa later may be good and perhaps Cameron has been able to find out more about the texts. Things seem to be happening in Wetherby, just what I'm not sure but there are definitely undercurrents.

## Chapter Six

Pippa had sounded quite down in the dumps when I rang her last night. Apparently, Cameron is waiting for another member of the Police Department in Leeds to get back to him by this morning. She has promised to call me as soon as he lets her know anything. Part of the reason for her feeling so down last night was because the latest flame in her life had gone away for business reasons and would be away until the end of the week. Good riddance as far as I am concerned. Pippa was not sure where he had gone but it had something to do with the restaurant trade. According to lover boy Antonio, he owns a large restaurant in Aranjuez, near the palace gardens. When I have more time, I think I will do a little checking, but my business comes first.

Flossie loves to ride alongside me whilst I go buying stock for Crumbs. She loves to go to the farm not far from Wetherby where I buy all my free-range eggs for baking. In another world it would be wonderful to be able to just go into the garden and get fresh eggs each morning from my own hens. Perhaps one day when I have somewhere in the countryside. It's only 7 am so these eggs will be ultra fresh, I hope they have cooled down!

"Hello Joe, how are the hens doing? I'd better take five trays today please, then we have plenty for all the extra cakes I need to bake."

"Business booming, eh?" Joe said in his gravelly voice.

"It is for now with all the curious customers after my recent celebrity status. You know what they say, today's news is tomorrow's fish and chip paper."

"It is that lass, you just take care."

"I'll try Joe, you too."

Back in the car with Flossie happy after her visit sniffing all around the farm, my phone is singing its 'coffee calypso' tune in my shoulder bag. Caller ID shows my friend Al from Miro café in Leeds is calling.

"Hello Al, how are you?"

"Kate, thank goodness I got hold of you, I don't know what to do, what should I do?" Al gabbled.

"Al, you haven't told me what is wrong yet."

"Oh no, oh Kate, it's a body, here, here in the back, outside the back door wedged below the steps. A woman."

"Al, is she breathing?" I asked trying to sound calm but inside my heart is thumping. Two of us in less than two weeks surrounded by bodies and both of us café owners.

"No. I can see her through the glass, all crumpled and her eyes, her eyes staring upwards, staring Kate, wide open, just staring, it's horrible. There's a lot of blood from her head all down her face, what the hell shall I do, what the hell shall I do! God this is terrible I can't look, she's staring at me Kate, help me please!"

"Al, call the police and whatever you do, don't touch anything, just close the front of the shop and sit down until they arrive, got that?"

"Yes Kate, right thank you."

"Don't forget to also ring Nariman, so he doesn't park his car in the back. Text him instead then keep your phone free in case the police try to call you back. Al, did you hear me?"

Al sounds panicky, he's making stressful noises and using a lot of strong language. I can imagine him stomping up and down the shop floor, phone to his ear whilst running his other hand through his now almost non-existent hair. When he is stressed, he tends to swear but not in front of his customers, the kitchen gets the brunt of it, or Nariman and vice versa.

"Let me know by text later and I will try to get to you when Sally has arrived at Crumbs to take over from me. Al, Al, breathe slowly, right now ring the police, okay?"

"I will, thank you Kate." Al rang off.

Miro café is ideally situated opposite the Parkinson steps of the University of Leeds. They get very busy with the students and lecturers, always open, always welcoming. Café Miro was our meeting place for a good coffee and girly chat from the age of 14 until I moved to Wetherby. Al and Nariman put up with our girlish shrieks and laughter and non-stop talking. They became our friends and sometimes weekend employers. I don't know yet exactly what has happened, I just know how numbing it feels to be involved in murder. Coming across a body chills your whole being and fills your thoughts day and night.

Back in Crumbs I feel as though I am working on automatic pilot going through all the jobs needing to be completed before opening up. Perhaps some music will help. I'll turn the radio on whilst washing up the few baking items I have used.

"Good morning this is the 8:00 AM news. The body of a woman has been found in the parking area of a café opposite the University of Leeds. As yet the police have not been able to identify the woman. The price of fruit and vegetables is..."

I switched it off with the words spinning in my head. How awful for Al and Nariman. I usually park in the back car park whenever I get the chance to visit them. The café is below street level both front and back. An iron staircase goes down from the car park at the back to a very narrow passage and the big glass window and door of the kitchen. Electric metal shutters are pulled down at closing time for security. At the front there are a few tables and benches at street level with steps going down to a narrow seating area surrounded by pots of colourful plants and the glass door entrance to Miro. Streets of student occupied terrace houses look onto the back car park of Miro but it's usually dark and deserted at night, nobody would see anything going on. I can't get my head around why there, other than someone knew how dark it is and had the opportunity. When I see Al, I need to ask more.

"Flossie what is going on? First me finding the body at the University sports hall then Al at Miro, they are five minutes' walk from each other but have no connection at all. Is murder following us around?"

Flossie is shaking her head for "no".

"I think I'd better ring Mr Potter and see if he can help out this afternoon so I can go and check on Al and Nariman."

"Woof."

Bless him, that's all arranged, a quick tiddle for both Flossie and myself and then it's time to open up again. Whoops! Nearly forgot to put the float money in the till, okay done.

Blinds are up, the sign on the door turned and all the top small windows open for fresh air. It's a little breezy today so customers will close the door behind them if I leave it open, some seem to hate fresh air.

"Don't do it Kitty my dear," Rose spoke from who knows where behind the counter. "Don't get involved this time."

"I'm not getting involved. How can I when I don't know anything about it other than a friend needs to talk to me?"

"Oh, Kitty my dear, we both know better than that. This could be dangerous again."

"Then help me, that's if you can. They are good people who will be terribly affected by all that has happened through no fault of their own. I just want to support them, there's no harm in that."

"None at all my dear but I can only watch over you and I need to be in Rome quite soon. We are all meeting up by the Trevi fountain and I am so looking forward to seeing my old friends."

"What about Gran? When will she be able to come through or meet up with you? She has been up there a little time before you and I'm still waiting." Right now I could do with my Gran, her love and advice.

"Have patience my dear, I'll tell you when she has gained strength to be able to do it all. I really must go now Kitty. Flossie, watch her, you know how stubborn and inquisitive she is."

"Woof," Flossie barked, walking behind the counter with her tail wagging furiously.

"What do you reckon Flossie, how am I going to get involved because I really don't particularly want to? Honestly Flossie, I can't see that this has anything to do with me other than supporting friends through it. There are enough odd things going on here in Wetherby without getting involved in more murders in Leeds."

Flossie cocked her head to one side and winced, so I take it she's not convinced either.

Sally has just taken six hot buttered crumpets

to a table in the garden with three young girls sitting together chatting and giggling away. One is playing mother by pouring the tea for them all. That's just how my friends and I were, not a care in the world if it didn't involve makeup, boys and celebrity gossip. School? For me it came low on the list, I survived. It's totally different these days, the pressure on young ones is far more than then. Sometimes I really feel for them.

"Lost in thought," a familiar voice broke through my memories and the clean manly smell of the original Imperial Leather soap engulfed me. He is literally taking my breath away Mills and Boon style!

"Oh, just remembering my own youth and times like that with my friends," I said, pointing to the girls in the garden who were now showing photos on their phones of boys they had met, I can tell by their expressions who they really liked. Happy days. "How is it going for Pippa?"

"Not much we can do I'm afraid. The techie says it's a pay as you go phone. To be honest the messages are not abusive or threatening in any way. They appear more concerned about her than anything else. Unless the tone alters that's all we can do. She knows she can contact me if anything changes, sorry I can't help further Kate."

"I understand, it's odd that's all but then a lot of things are odd at the moment. Can I ask you what, if anything, you know about the murder at Café Miro, Leeds?" Well, there's no harm in asking is there?

"Murder? How do you know it's murder?" Cameron queried with his eyebrows up.

"Oh, come on Cameron. Al, the owner, rang me when he pulled up his metal shutter and was face to face with the poor soul. Her twisted body and staring eyes gave him a terrible shock. Besides, down a narrow, damp, dark passageway at the bottom of all those steps is not your usual place to end your days, whatever the reason." I can feel goosebumps on my arms and that's nothing to do with how close Cameron is beside me. That could have been me not so long ago, but I survived.

"You're shivering Kate, this is too soon for you, don't get involved, please."

Why is everyone saying the same? Friends are friends, that's all there is to this horrible situation.

"The owners and I go back a very long way. If I can help them, I will. If it's murder, neither of them had anything to do with it."

"How can you be so sure Kate? People react in peculiar ways when pushed. You can never know someone fully, circumstances change. I've known the gentlest of men commit murder on the spur of the moment."

"So it was murder then."

Cameron isn't answering, he's just looking straight into my eyes full of concern. "I'm saying it because I know you."

"You just said how you can never know someone fully." Oops! That was too prickly and unfair of me. "I'm sorry Cameron. That was uncalled for, I will be careful."

"Fair enough, call me if you need to talk." his voice sounded a little hurt but at least he managed a smile.

The scene at Café Miro is so familiar. Blue and white crime scene tape at the front and back of the shop. Police forensic vans and investigation team vans parked outside. It's teeming with police, some in full white suits taking photos in the backyard. Most of the back street is taped off with police guarding the top and bottom of the street. I just managed to find a parking spot on the road at the front of the café and attract Al's attention through the windows. The policeman on guard at the front is sticking to his orders and refusing to let me down the steps, fairs fair, until Al said I am expected, and family, sort of.

Inside Miro it's slightly calmer. Al and Nariman, although stressed and concerned about the situation, seemed to be keeping busy supplying drinks and food to those on duty. The phone is ringing but nobody is answering it.

"We can't answer, it's always the newspapers and television people," Nariman said, reading my mind.

"Of course, how are you both?" This time it's me giving the hugs to someone in shock.

"Al has taken the brunt of it. We are just trying to keep busy but apart from all you see we will be alright. Better than the poor woman Al found." Nariman wiped his overheated brow with a serviette and made the three of us some coffee.

"Did you know or recognise her Al?" hoping in my heart she wasn't a regular customer, that would really hit them hard if she had been.

"Not know her, but we both recognised her. She only came in yesterday for the first time, we've never seen her before that."

"What was she like? Friendly, quiet, did you see her with anyone? I'm sorry I know the police will have asked you everything, but sometimes small things come to you much later in the day."

I looked at Nariman who put his hands up in the air, "I was in the kitchen and could only see her at the counter while she ordered with Al. Small, long dark hair, foreign looking, nicely dressed in a cerise dress with a navy blue and cerise pashmina, gold earrings, no rings and strangely no handbag."

"Wow Nariman that's very observant for a brief encounter from the kitchen. I bet the detective was pleased with you." Well, I was impressed even if no one else was.

"With my wife and daughter, you get used to it!" Nariman said with a half-smile. "No, the detective looked at me with more suspicion than appreciation."

"What did you think Al?" Al always appreciates a pretty face but not in any pervy way, he's just one of those men who is very at ease talking to both men and women, mostly women.

"She ordered a latte and a sandwich, piri-piri chicken and mozzarella cheese, spice and nice!" Al gave one of his cheeky grins. "I think she was Spanish; she didn't seem familiar with our currency."

"What gave you that impression when she ordered a latte not a Spanish coffee as you may expect?"

"Not all Spaniards who come in here order Spanish coffee. We have one who only drinks tea. She took a 20 pound note out of a small pink purse she had in her hand. She sat on the sofa by the door but stood up again and walked over to look at the Miro posters. Her face changed, she seemed to know them and smiled as she looked over them all." Al looked thoughtfully at the posters. "I've just remembered something. When she walked to the posters, I glanced up. Oh, come on Kate you know I appreciate a pretty woman," Al's hands went up as we laughed. "I noticed her feet, well particularly one foot in her sandals, okay Nariman so I like feet! Stop putting me off. Kate, there was a slight gap between her big toe and the next, just slight, on her right foot."

"Interesting Al, I'm sure it will help them find who she is."

Miro café has three large, framed Miro posters on a long wall. I've never liked them, but Al loves them. He bought several many years ago, far too gaudy with exotic brush strokes and bright colours but at least they go with the café's name.

"Was she wearing the same outfit when you found her this morning?"

Al looked at Nariman and nodded, "Yes, but not the pashmina."

There goes the Miss Marple in me again and I promised!

There are two black leather sofas in Miro, one at the far end of the shop in an alcove by a large fridge and the counter. The sofa she sat on is in the entrance against a short wall facing a longer wall with the Miro posters on it. Tables and comfy chairs fill in the length of the shop to the counter at the top end. Glancing to the black sofa by the entrance door I can see it's not pushed back against the wall as it usually is.

"Have you been cleaning since the police checked in here earlier?"

"No, I haven't had the heart to. They didn't need to search inside the café as all the doors were locked and the two metal doors and window shutters down all night. I closed up last night and left by the front door and activated the shutters on that one as I went through it. She definitely was not there at 5:30 PM last night, I would have seen her. I always go to the bins with any rubbish before locking up and putting the shutters down, we both do." Al looks paler than before.

"Sit down Al, I'm bringing you a whisky, something stronger is needed for all of us,"

Nariman said, opening a cupboard door under the counter.

"Not for me thanks I'm driving," I smiled, remembering the countless end of day small tots of whatever was in the cupboard when the café doors had been locked up for the day. Always small glasses shared by the two friends as they went over the highs and lows of running a café.

Pulling the sofa further away from the wall I could see some navy-blue fringing peeping out from under the sofa. Nariman helped me pull it further away onto the shop floor. Underneath the sofa is the navy and cerise pink pashmina the mystery woman had been wearing while she had her coffee. She must have taken it off in the warmth of the café. Being silky it had somehow slid down the back and under the leather sofa onto the tiled flooring.

"Don't touch it Al. Please can I have some gloves and one of your plastic carrier bags. We need to bag it and give it to the police."

Al brought the carrier bag and some gloves. As I picked it up and put it inside the bag a waft of something unfamiliar hit me. I should train Flossie in this! I also noticed two or three of the loops which made the fringe are missing.

"Kate! What is it with you and bodies?"

Oh no, why does the only decent man around have to be here of all places. I'm in for another telling off.

"Hello Detective Sergeant Benson, I could say

the same for you." I'm trying to sound cheerful. Why is he back working in Leeds? They cover far too many miles.

"It's my job Kate and we are short of staff, so we are pulled everywhere."

"These are my friends, Al and Nariman," I said, introducing them to Cameron. "Al found the lady this morning and we just found this behind the sofa, it's what she was wearing yesterday." I held up the bag and Cameron took it from me.

"Thank you, I need to speak to these gentlemen so perhaps you should say your goodbyes now Kate. I will call you when I can," Cameron said, moving to the door and holding it open.

Charming! I hugged my friends and whispered into Al's ear for them to call me.

"Goodbye detective," I said with more than a little sarcasm in my tone. "You may want to consider the fact she came into the café with only a purse not a handbag."

"Meaning what exactly?" he asked sternly.

"Meaning the possibility of her living in one of these flats above the shops, this street is full of flats." I pointed to the numerous windows above each café opposite the University of Leeds. "Merely an observation detective, goodbye." I turned and climbed the steps to the pavement my face on fire with anger, men!

# Chapter Seven

My ride back to Wetherby did not improve my angry reaction to Cameron's dismissal of me like a naughty school child. I know he has his work to do but I may have been able to help him knowing the area from childhood, though that's his loss.

Crumbs has quite a few customers inside and several enjoying drinks and cake in the garden. Mr Greaves is sitting in the corner with his usual order, untouched. Sally is busy slicing cake and putting them on a cake stand with its glass dome covering the cake slices.

"Everything alright?" I asked, jerking my head in Mr Greaves' direction.

"Not sure," she answered quietly. "He's been like that for at least 15 minutes now."

I nodded and made my way through the tables to Mr Greaves.

"Hello Mr Greaves, would you like me to make you some fresh tea?"

Mr Greaves looked up almost in shock as I broke through his silence. "Err, um, oh haven't I drunk it yet? I'm sorry I was lost in thought," he said apologetically.

"Then let me get you some more, I think you

need a good strong tea to revive you."

"You are kind, thank you very much," he said, running his hand around his face.

Returning with a fresh pot of tea and a clean cup and saucer I can hear his phone beeping. Mr Greaves is reading the text message and I can see his hand shaking.

"Are you sure you're alright? Let me pour you some tea, take a sip, you look as though you have seen a ghost." I automatically looked around as I said it, almost expecting Rose to be visible which is impossible of course, well I think it is.

"I'm sorry, yes please," Mrs Greaves said taking four cubes of sugar from the bowl and stirring frantically. I didn't think he took sugar, so something has upset him. He quickly cancelled the text and put his phone away.

"Just a disturbing text, a hoax I expect," he said, trying to smile.

"Wetherby must be having an epidemic of hoax calls and texts. Don't ever click onto any links or they will have every penny from you." By the look on his face, I have hit on a sore point. If I do speak to Cameron, which for the sake of Mr Greaves I will, then it will have to be mentioned.

Time flies by when you are busy and boy, I have been very busy. My eyes are burning with tiredness and my feet don't belong to me they ache so much with standing. Crumbs is closed, everything has been cleaned and prepared for tomorrow and the day's takings are safely stashed away. I still have not heard from my friends at Miro or Cameron, but I really did not expect to hear from the great detective yet. As soon as the timer goes off and the cakes are out of the oven cooling, I'm out of here for a walk with Flossie. That's it, perfect timing and even if I say so myself these cakes are pretty perfect too.

"Ready Flossie?"

"Woof."

I love walking along by the river and so it seems do a lot of locals this evening. Flossie has had lots of meet and greet sniffing to do which never fails to amuse me. Thank goodness humans don't greet each other the same way, so embarrassing!

"Hello Stan, how is Agnes? Are her bunions still hurting as much?"

"Not so bad today lass, but she's at home looking after the grandkids. I'm out for some peace and a pint with Burt."

"Well say hello to them both from me please."

"Will do lass, that pint is going to last me a good long time, at least 'til the son in law picks them up," said Stan winking. Stan loves his family but as well as him and Burt keeping the streets and bins of the town centre and riverfront clean and tidy, he seems to babysit a lot.

Turning and walking back alongside the river under the bridge towards the weir, I can see Mr Greaves and Susan Walsh the postmistress mistress on a bench. I'm no body language expert but she looks mad with her hands stabbing the evening air left and right. She has her phone out and so has Mr Greaves. He still looks worried. The problem is this is the only path and one of them is bound to spot us. Spotted!

Susan has jumped up and marched off towards the weir and Mr Greaves is standing, slowly flexing his right leg before moving off in the same direction.

"Did you see that, Flossie?"

"Woof."

"I don't believe in coincidences, do you?"

Flossie is shaking her head from side to side.

I've just gone in through my garden gate, turned the key in the lock of my kitchen door and my phone has started its tune. It's Cameron, Whoopee!

"Hello."

"Hello Kate, are you home?"

"Just walking into the kitchen. Where are you, still in Leeds?"

"Actually, I'm looking through your shop window. Fancy a coffee and an apology?"

Now that has made me smile. "Always good to see a man grovel. Coffees are on me."

I unlocked the door with a stupid grin on my face. Apologies given and accepted, coffee and cake eaten and now the conversation is getting more serious.

"You were right about the shawl."

"Pashmina," I said smiling.

"Still a shawl, a posh one. It was hers and you were right about her not living far away because of the purse."

"How near?"

"Above Café Miro, that's how near. A flat on the top floor being used by people not staying long."

"Like an Airbnb place," I said nodding.

"Similar, we will know more when we can get hold of the landlord who seems to be away at the moment. Nobody saw her arrive or spoke to her except for your friends Al and Nariman." Cameron poured out more coffee and slowly stirred in some cream. "You asked how she was killed," he said, offering to pour some cream for me.

"No thanks, I prefer hot milk," I said, reaching for my small jug of hot milk. "I didn't ask because I was hoping you would tell me whatever you can."

"Right. Well, no name as yet, not sure of her nationality, could be Spanish, 40s, not much luggage just a holdall. No passport in the holdall or in her handbag which was empty, no ID at all. Cause of death was blunt force trauma with a brick which we found with her blood on it thrown in the backyard of Miro. Forensics are still working there."

"I saw some bricks had broken away from the wall attached to Miro's high gateposts. It's the shop next to them who have not rebuilt it. Poor soul she must have been attacked when she was going through the backyard up to the flat. Seems strange going down a dark backstreet to get into the flat when it was so much easier to enter from the entrance on the main road, opposite the

University. Do you think she walked or was driven there, and did she have her purse with her?" I had not heard him mention a purse.

"Purse, no I don't think so. That could have been taken by whoever followed and attacked her. What are you thinking Kate? I can practically see the wheels of your brain in your head."

"Just that we have a lady who pops out with only a purse for coffee and then later goes out in a strange city without a handbag or her phone, anything at all. It doesn't sit right with me. I'm visiting Madrid soon and I will want something with me at all times, for safety."

"Mmm, I see your point. Forensics will have checked the yard but if your friends are in and out with cars, we will have to see."

"Al doesn't drive and Nariman didn't get there until after the police, so he parked at the front."

"Good."

"Also, someone must have gone into the flat and removed all her personal items. To me that's not just a thief, that's more."

Cameron smiled. "You are overthinking Kate, remember."

"Alright I know. Any more to do with Pippa?" I'm trying to change the topic, my reasoning being not to push too far in the hope of more info later.

"Not yet and as we are splitting ourselves in two with staff off sick and on leave, I'm afraid it will have to wait, I'm sorry."

I decided to update him on the other epidemic of

strange messages. At least he can never say he was not told. He looks tired as he listens but before he can comment his phone starts ringing. Cameron's brows went up as he drank the dregs of his coffee quickly saying he was on his way. I walked over and unlocked the café door before he could say anything. His hand shut up.

"Don't ask, Kate."

"I won't."

"Thanks for the coffee and cake," he smiled a tired, weak smile.

"You know where I am, anytime." Oh well I can live in hope.

When he had gone, I suddenly felt quite lonely. This is what living with a policeman must be like. A wet nose is nuzzling my hand and Flossie's warm body is leaning into me, as she often does, bliss.

"I know Flossie, you're always here for me aren't you girl?"

"Woof."

"So am I my dear even though you ignore my warnings."

"Rose, you sound like gypsy Rose Lee in a fortune teller's tent at Blackpool."

"Be serious Kate, you are doing it again, playing Miss Marple. You haven't even booked your hotel yet. Get it booked and keep out of trouble, please Kate."

"Rose I really have not had the time to think about Madrid, which doesn't mean I won't." Damn I wish I knew where I could look when answering her. I'm looking towards my fridge because her voice sounds as though she is sitting on the top of it. Is there enough room for her? I don't know, perhaps ghosts pack up small when they need to.

"Over here Kitty not there, no, over by the dishwasher. By the way my dear you really must give this machine a clean through, it's starting to whiff."

"It does not whiff!" For all I know ghosts can't smell, they can't eat so it's possible they can't smell. A reminder to myself to consult my ghost manual on what senses ghosts still have whilst floating around.

"Your policeman young man always smells nice. Your Gran will approve of him as he uses her favourite soap, Imperial Leather."

"Rose you haven't!" I had a dreadful thought of Rose invading Cameron's privacy in his shower.

"Indeed, my dear, indeed."

"I thought there was a ghost law against spying in someone's house."

"It's not spying, I was merely observing, for your sake my dear nothing else."

"Really? As Gran always said Rose, tell it to the marines"

Rose chuckled and suddenly my kitchen became still again.

## Chapter Eight

Most of my day is spent rushing around. If it's not shopping for supplies, it's clearing tables and serving or baking. Would I swap it for a highly paid job with benefits? Easy answer, no. One of the things Gran drilled into me was that in life there is no such thing as a free meal, everything comes with a catch.

Flossie is my driving companion as we journey back to Leeds with a long list to buy from Costco. Croissants and Danish pastries I do not make myself or fruited tea cakes and crumpets for toasting. These are easy to buy in bulk at the warehouse and put in one of the freezers. Yorkshire folk love them in the morning or afternoon with a cuppa.

It's a journey which frustrates me at the best of times because of the road and the speed limits. One minute you're travelling at 50 mph the next you have to drop to 30. Police cars can be parked up driveways ready to pounce on drivers going over the 30 mph speed limit.

"Watch out for the police Flossie and keep me at 30 please. This hill is ridiculous and such a long drag dropping from 50 to 30 uphill."

"Woof."

Coming back from Leeds it's all downhill and drivers usually go over the speed limit even when driving on their brakes, that's when the police swoop, like birds of prey.

"How are you doing Flossie? This is the bit I detest, driving through Scarcroft. Well! Look at that idiot coming down the hill, he's bombing along, now he deserves to be stopped and prosecuted."

"Woof."

It's a dark blue Volvo with the driver on his mobile. The driver's window is down and my goodness in that speedy flash by I'm sure the reckless idiot is Antonio. Now I do doubly hope he gets stopped and fined, but his kind never do. Note to self to contact Pippa and see if he is back then it will confirm my suspicions.

When I go shopping with a list you can bet your life I come back with twice as much. My excuse is it's a long way to go and you never know when you will need it. As there is only me running the café, I don't get any objections.

Home again. If only I'd had more time, I could have checked in at Miro and seen if they know anything yet. Perhaps the police are still around so maybe it's best I stay away, Cameron seems to find out everything, spies are everywhere.

Sally helped me put my eight bags of shopping

away without commenting. Although the sun is shining it seems fairly quiet in Crumbs and the customers we do have are quite content to sit back and chat for a while. Sally looks extra tired today and I do feel guilty leaving her on her own so much.

"Let's have a drink Sally, you sit down I'll get them." We have a couple of chairs in the kitchen for us and we can see through to the shop if anyone should arrive. It's not often we get the chance to sit but I think she needs to.

"Are you alright Sally?"

Her eyes have dark circles underneath them.

"I'm alright or I will be if I can get some sleep. The two youngest had nightmares last night, my eldest told them ghost stories, which they loved at the time. Halloween will be horrendous, with my brood they're either hyped up or scared to death."

"I know the feeling." The problem is at my age and living with a ghost the nightmares are still happening, bless her. "Go home and get some rest before they all come home from school, go on I can manage."

"Are you sure? I could really do with even half an hour or so, thanks Kate," Sally said, hugging me long and hard.

"I'll go through the CV's tonight and then we'll contact some of the kids who want part time work, schools will be finishing soon."

"Thanks again, bye," Sally said grabbing her bag and cardigan.

As it's fairly quiet I decided to wash some shelves. Starting with my teapot shelf. They look so pretty all lined up on this shelf above my baking equipment cupboard. It may seem odd to some people, but I like to arrange them in order of pattern and colour, not that it bothers me if it doesn't stay that way.

"Hello there," a familiar female voice called out.

"Oh, I am sorry Susan, I was taking advantage of our quiet spell. What can I get you?"

Susan Walsh must be having an afternoon off today from the Post Office. She looks in need of something strong and refreshing.

"Coffee today please and please may I have some hot milk on the side. I don't know how strong I will need it. That date and walnut cake looks very tempting, go on I'll have some please."

"One of my favourites too but I am trying to cut down on what I eat. It's amazing how the weight goes on just smelling it all as it bakes. Sit and relax Susan, I won't be long with your order."

"Thank you, Kate," Susan's tone sounds flat.

"Here you are, tell me if you need any more hot milk, enjoy."

"This is wonderful, thank you Kate."

I watched from the kitchen as she poured coffee from her cafetière adding just a drop of milk, that will be strong, but it looks needed. One task completed and I'm feeling pretty good with myself. Gran always said, "Don't put off until tomorrow as tomorrow may never come." I always thought, well if it doesn't, I won't have to worry about anything! I was a lot younger than.

Girlish giggles from the shop floor made me spin around and walk out of the kitchen. Not teenagers, it's Pippa snuggling up close to that slimeball Antonio. Ugh! He's pecking her on her neck, yuck, yuck not in my presence please!

"Can I help you?" I asked Pippa whilst I glared at him with a sudden vision of Dracula diving in to suck Pippa's lifeblood. He makes my skin crawl! What on earth does she see in him? He certainly looks the part with highly polished tan shoes, his crisp beige linen trousers, dark blue linen jacket and a dazzling white shirt open at the neck showing a very tanned torso. Don't want to think about it! That hair is 100% dyed at his age, strewth I've got grey on the top at 30.

Pippa broke herself free from his well-manicured tentacles and thrust her left hand forward, not that I could have missed it. On her wedding finger the plain wedding band from her last marriage was gone and, in its place, a large square cut ruby flanked either side by a nice sized diamond. Not my cup of tea or coffee but a girl can get used to something that big.

My face must have registered shock. My eyes have grown wider, and my jaw feels as though it has dropped several centimetres.

"Aren't you going to congratulate me? I know it's a surprise to me too. Antonio just got back today and proposed," Pippa said while Slimeball stroked her arm.

I opened my mouth to speak but the crash of Susan Walsh's cup falling and breaking on the floor next to us cut me off. Coffee and several fragments of a pretty Royal Albert cup scattered all around our feet. Susan jumped up; her face turned as white as the fine china cup in pieces on the floor.

"Are you alright Susan, it didn't fall on your foot, did it?" I asked her.

"Oh, I'm so sorry Kate, I will pay for the cup," she said shakily.

"Not at all please don't worry. Why don't you go and sit in the garden, and I will bring you some fresh coffee." I got her arm and walked her through the door to the garden.

"You are so kind Kate."

"Relax and I will be out soon." Something has my antennae activated and I intend to find out why.

"I'm sorry Pippa, that spoilt your moment so please let me see your ring again." Pippa held out her hand, beaming from ear to ear. I wish I could feel happy for her, but I can't.

"Wow, that's a nice chunk of a ruby and you didn't know anything at all, what a surprise." I tried to be kind.

"I didn't know anything until an hour ago. Antonio is such a romantic he bought it in Newcastle this week and I think it's gorgeous." Pippa glowed as she spoke, moving her hand from side to side so the diamond sparkled more in the light. Newcastle my foot, I don't think so. Smile Kate, for Pippa's sake.

"Coffee to celebrate?" I asked, but only so I could find out more.

"If you wish my darling, my time is all yours, forever," Antonio replied for them both as he slobbered all over her hand.

As I prepared coffee for Susan and the love birds, I cut some black cherry and almond cake keeping my eyes peeled on him as I did. My goodness he makes me cringe.

"Here you are Susan, are you alright?"

"I am now thank you I just feel incredibly embarrassed. Flossie has come to help me by letting me stroke her ears. I think she understands how silly I feel," Susan continued stroking Flossie.

"Oh, she understands for sure. Sorry I have to serve the love birds I will see you soon," I said, winking at Flossie who I swear winked back.

Antonio stood up as I approached with the tray and smiling his white toothed (at least they have that in common) slimy grin he took the tray from me. I wanted to slap him! I just could not bring myself to thank him so I'm sorry Rose for not having any manners.

"Do you go to Newcastle often?" I asked, delving.

"Yes, I do, usually for three to four days every month for business."

"Pippa hasn't had time to tell me anything, what kind of business is that?" Come on Slimeball tell me more.

"The restaurant business. I have one in Spain," he answered.

"How lovely, you obviously have a lot of good staff to run it."

"Why?" he said with an edge to his tone of voice.

"I know how difficult it can be, and you have been away for quite some time." I tried to sound light-hearted and smiled.

"It's one of the reasons why I pay my manager well."

"Of course. I'm supposed to be booking a hotel in Madrid for the weekend. I've been looking online at the Hotel Emperador; do you happen to know it? My mother wants me to go for a break, she is paying as a gift for my birthday."

His eyebrows twitched slightly when I said the name of the hotel and by his body language, I'd say he knows it well.

"No, I don't get to Madrid, so I haven't had the pleasure of such a good hotel."

He's lying through his dyed black hair! I need to speak to Pippa and ask where he is from and find out more about his restaurant. Thankfully a party of six ladies have just come in chattering and laughing together. Saved by the ladies!

"Excuse me Pippa duty calls, I will call you when I can, bye."

"Goodbye Kate and thank you again for the coffee and cake," Pippa said cheerfully.

Mr Slimeball never spoke so I don't see the need to acknowledge him either, but he is now on my delving list for sure.

Each time I think about going online to look at flights or the hotel something seems to stop me. I firmly believe it's for a reason no matter what Rose or Carol may say, this time it was Al phoning me.

"How are you both?" I asked full of concern as this is not as usual cheery voice.

"Oh, you know, getting there," Al said in a flat voice.

"Have you been busy? People never fail to amaze me. Crumbs was a crazy place after my problems."

"Same here really. I rang because I need to tell you about what we have just found out, it may be something or nothing at all."

"I'm all ears Al."

"You know Fag Ash Lil who lives at the back, first terrace house on the row facing our backyard?"

"Yes, I know her." Everybody knows Lil, she has lived there for centuries. Lil is seldom seen without a cigarette dangling from her lower lip, the ash getting longer and longer. No matter what she is doing the cigarette dangles from her pleated nicotine-stained lips. Lil has never been known to drop it, even when she is shouting at the students for making too much noise. Fag Ash Lil is a big woman with an even bigger voice. All the local drug dealers and thugs fear her. Rumour has it she was once married to a little man who went out after the 1966 World Cup to get her 10 Park Drive cigarettes and never came back. The next day she paved her small backyard. If that were today, I'd be watching her like a hawk. Wives do occasionally kill husbands, look at the Victorians.

"Lil came to our back door today and told us she saw a dark car drop a female off and she went through the yard next door and into the flats. It was dark and she doesn't know cars. It was parked in the road, so she didn't see the driver as he stayed in the car."

"When was that Al, did she remember?"

"The night before she came in for coffee. So, two nights before the morning I found her dead."

"Have you told Detective Benson? You have his card, give him a call. That information could be relevant to the case and I'm sure he will want to speak to Lil. Let me know if anything else happens or if I can help you in anyway. Love to you both."

"Will do Kate, take care," Al said more cheerfully.

Mr Potter has arrived for his usual and then a bit of gardening, but he is quite happy to take over for a few minutes whilst I check on Susan in the garden. It's unusually quiet today but I have to say it's helping me out.

"How are you now Susan? Do you want me to get you anything else?"

"I'm fine thank you. Flossie and I are firm friends now and honestly Kate she has helped me feel calm again. I really don't know what happened in there, but it has passed."

"Flossie is a miracle, I wouldn't be without her, would I my lovely girl?"

Flossie shook her head from side to side for "no".

Okay I'm going to bite the bullet and dive straight in with my questioning. I have to as it's burning away in my head, so fingers crossed Susan doesn't react badly.

"What do you think to Pippa's news then? She said it was quite unexpected." My eyes are scanning her for any adverse signs but so far so good.

Susan shrugged her shoulders, "I hope she knows what she is getting involved in."

"What do you mean, do you know him already Susan?" I saw her flinch as I asked the question. She knows him, I'd stake my café on it.

"No, no," she stammered far too quickly.

"Then like Flossie you must be picking up some bad vibes from him. I know I do. If my Gran were here, she would say if you don't like being alongside someone it's because your auras are clashing so stay away. My Gran and Rose were very spiritual. Perhaps that's it." Little does she know Rose still is, and in this very café too!

"Perhaps it is. Pippa obviously thinks he is wonderful the way she hangs on to his every word. Words are cheap and she has been swept away by his charms, just like all the others." Susan looked sad again.

Interesting she should say "like all the others". That to me proves she knows of him at least. Probably the best thing for me to do at the moment is to hold my tongue, bide my time.

"Stay as long as you need with Flossie, and I will see you soon." I smiled my reassuring smile, but Flossie knows as she's winking at me again.

# Chapter Nine

Sleep had not come so easily last night. When my 6:00 AM alarm pierced through my brain I felt I had run a marathon. Running and gyms are not for me, I couldn't even run for a bus. My PE classes at school often had me hiding in the disused shower cubicles for the lesson, that or pleading monthly cramps. My teacher didn't seem to mind, in fact it made her life easier when it came to forming teams as nobody wanted me on their team letting them down. I guess we had an unspoken understanding with the usual "must try harder" on my report.

Flossie is sweeping the floor with her tail waiting patiently for a small corner of a freshly baked scone.

"It's still too hot Flossie my darling, we don't want to upset your tummy. Don't let Rose know or I will be in trouble again, here I'll blow on it."

Flossie grinned at me as I blew on the small bit of scone and gave it to her. I'm sure she just swallows everything whole no matter how big it is.

"There, that's the evidence disposed of."

"Woof."

"Really Kitty, if you think you can fool me then

you have learnt nothing through the years," Rose shrilled in her prim and proper voice.

"Oh, oh" I said to Flossie, rolling my eyes.

"Don't roll your eyes Kitty, it's very unbecoming at your age. I came from an important meeting to have a word with you," Rose said crossly.

"I'm sorry Rose what do you want to say to me?"

"I know how much you want to help your friends and I know you are more than capable of looking after yourself. You are, I don't tell you because I don't want to encourage you but Kitty this is very dangerous."

"Rose, if you know so much why can't you tell me? My mind is full of all sorts of bits of information but it's like a jigsaw puzzle with half the pieces missing, will I find them and finish the puzzle?"

"You will and that's what I am afraid of my dear, you are chasing danger. I can only try to protect you nothing more. Are you going to Madrid? Perhaps you will find what you are looking for there."

"Rose I'm not looking for another man, that's not top of my wish list."

"Not at the moment as your mind is elsewhere and anyway the one for you is right under your nose and you can't see it," Rose said softly.

"Where? There's only Mr Potter and forgive me but he is more your age than mine. Do you have relationships up there? Wow, that's something I never thought of until now."

"I'm not answering that Kitty and I don't have the time for this kind of conversation. I have to fly back to Istanbul straight away."

"What trouble are you causing in Istanbul may I ask?"

"They're trying to exorcise one of their residents in the Sekerci Erol café/patisserie. She has been there for decades, it's not right. My friends have told me how she may scare a few customers, but she doesn't throw anything, and I know plenty of ghosts who do."

"How many are flying in for the meeting and what can you do when you can't be seen?" This is all so incredible I'm trying to visualise a ghostly sit in, it's impossible.

"There will be as many as we can pack into the café and the rest outside. Whoever is doing the exorcism will be sorry they took it on by the time we have finished. It will be worse than any horror film, I promise."

"So, when you scare him to death, literally, then he becomes one of you and he will know what it feels like to be made homeless. It figures but then I do have a very vivid imagination."

"Goodness me Kitty, we will not go that far my dear. Must fly, please just book your trip before Carol gets on her high horse about it. Take care my dear."

"Goodbye Rose wherever you are," I said into the air, but instinct tells me she has already flown.

As days go this has been a good one. Friendly

customers both regulars and new ones enjoying the best that Crumbs can offer. Sadly, none of the ones I wanted to see came by. Pippa, Mr Greaves and Susan must all be too busy for a cuppa and cake. The other productive thing I have managed to do is arrange for more help in Crumbs, not before time.

Sally comes from a big family which always amazes me how many seem to still live around Wetherby. Two of her nieces (twins) need part time jobs and in my mind, they will be good, especially as Sally will be here to watch them. Perhaps I will be able to book my trip for next weekend once they have been trained up. There is a lot to think about before then. I must try on some of my summer clothes and book the hairdressers as I promised, well my own hairdressers not a poncey one as Carol wanted.

Walking helps me to think things through and I have managed to do a lot of thinking whilst walking with Flossie alongside the river. Something I can't shake off is how I feel about Pippa's latest man who I now think of as Mr Slimeball. It wouldn't harm to phone her as I'm sure she will be so excited to share news with me, it's certainly worth a try. Cameron is also on my mind but it's awkward, I don't want to bother him when he is so busy. Gosh! Why didn't I think of it before? I could do what Rose said and try transferring some thoughts to him to prompt him into contacting me.

"What do you reckon Flossie, should I give it a whirl? Let's sit on this bench."

"Woof."

Right Kate close your eyes, think of Cameron, no think of him properly not like that! Wow, it's a good job all this is going on in my head and nobody can overhear me. Concentrate on Cameron in getting in touch, even better in person not by phone. Done! The proof of the pudding will be in the eating as Gran would have said.

"Woof."

"Good girl, come on let's go to the weir and walk back through the streets before it gets too dark."

"Woof."

We have walked past the flats and are just turning into the row of cottages where Mr Greaves lives. Glancing at my phone it's a little too early to see if another lady friend is leaving his home, shame but I'm too tired to walk for another half an hour. Tomorrow is one of the morning sessions at Crumbs for Miss Hall and Miss Winters, so all is not lost. I bet Miss Hall is looking out of her flat windows at us when we walk past, should I wave?

Raised angry voices met us as we rounded the corner so I've stopped dead before we can be seen.

"Wait here Flossie, let's use the hedge to hide behind whilst we see what's going on."

Flossie looked at me with a muffled "woof". Mr Greaves is shouting at a man who has got hold of his arm and seems to be pulling it. The man's right hand is raised with his fist clenched ready to punch Mr Greaves. This could be an attacker wanting money, I can't let it happen to Mr Greaves. I have to stop him. Bending down I've unclipped Flossie's lead.

"Go girl, get him!" I'm shouting. Flossie is charging down the street barking frantically and dives straight in for the kill. Jack Russells are feisty little dogs and once they get their teeth into something, boy do they hang on. Flossie has got him by the ankle and is going absolutely wild. I'm running the best I can, but I can see the man is trying to kick Flossie away from him.

"Stop kicking my dog you idiot!" I can't see who he is as he is wearing all black and a hat pulled down low over his face. "Leave him Flossie, let him go."

I can feel the panic in my heart in case he kicks her and injures her badly. It's not worth my dog getting the worst of it, much as I want to protect Mr Greaves, Flossie has to be protected as well. Flossie let go but is chasing after him back towards the weir barking loudly and snapping at his heels.

"Are you hurt, Mr Greaves? Who was he and what did he want, was it money?"

"I'm alright Kate thank you. Flossie saw him off and I really don't want a fuss," Mr Greaves said firmly.

"But we have to call the police, he was about to attack you I saw him. People can't go around doing that and getting away with it, let me ring for you."

"No! No! I don't want the police," he shouted.

"Go home Kate I just want to get into my own home and forget it happened." Mr Greaves turned and marched down his path and into his cottage, slamming his front door with a lot of force.

"Well, I didn't expect that outburst but maybe he is shocked after the attack," I said to Flossie who is panting at my feet. "I'm proud of you Flossie, are you sure you're not hurt by him, whoever that monster was?"

"Woof."

"Oh, my lovely little girl. If he had hurt you, I'd never forgive myself for sending you after him. Come on, let's go home for some special treats, just one more cuddle Flossie."

Flossie snuggled against my cheek so soft and warm. She has brought tears to my eyes. How could anyone hurt her? If I ever find out who he was he will be forever looking over his shoulder, the pig.

# Chapter Ten

Last night's aggressive attack on Mr Greaves and Flossie left me more shaken than I had realised. It even permeated my fitful dreams even though I forced myself out of one by waking up, only to return to the same dream. My eyes feel heavy with the lack of sleep, and I have a million and one things to deal with today.

"Let's have some music on the radio, Flossie to brighten the day up. I'll have a quick, hot shower then it's scrambled eggs on toast, fancy some?"

"Woof."

"Good job I baked treble the amount of scones yesterday. We can whip up some trays of buns after we have eaten and a couple of large sponges for decorating, the rest is in the freezer. Does that sound good girl?"

"Woof."

"This is this 6:00 AM news. Police in Leeds have not been able to identify the woman found murdered in the Woodhouse area near the University of Leeds earlier this week. If anyone has any information, please call Leeds City Police headquarters on 111 or contact Crimestoppers."

"Oh, Flossie that poor lady, she must be missed

by someone somewhere. I'd totally forgotten about Cameron and trying to contact him last night, looks like the thought transfer didn't work this time anyway. Why are you looking at me like that? Come on Flossie, I'm not Rose, and I don't have her powers, besides I'm shattered."

Flossie sighed, she did, a long sigh, then settled down with her paws crossed over her face. That is her way of giving up on a situation, if only I could do the same.

"Alright, alright I get the point. After my shower and food things will seem better, okay?"

"Woof."

The wonderful smell of baking always lifts my mood and I have to admit I did try Cameron again as the mixer was creaming the butter and sugar for the buns. With my luck he will get all the baking smells with the message and go to Cooplands bakery instead of here. Buns and cakes are out cooling, and I feel more awake now. Strawberries and raspberries are washed and draining ready for the cakes and the cream is in the mixer whipping gently to a lovely thicker, spreading consistency. Once everything is back in the fridge, I need to think about interviewing the twins and when I am actually going to go away to Madrid.

When I'm faced with umpteen things to do quickly, I become a list maker, it's the only way I can be semi organised. At this rate there will be a whole fridge door of lists. Gosh the hairdressers! What time is it? No, it's still too early to call Snips salon for an appointment, maybe I should check my wardrobe for a few clothes to pack, or maybe not, it could be depressing if they don't fit. No, it could all wait until tonight.

Flossie has been in the back garden, down to the bottom behind the shed for her tiddle, she likes to be private. I can hear her barking happily and here she comes with her little tail going faster than my windscreen wipers on full. If I had a tail, it would be wagging in time with hers, thank goodness I don't have one! Cameron is walking down the path stroking her head as she shamelessly nuzzles his leg, lucky girl! My word he is drop dead gorgeous as my friends and I used to say as teenagers, or sex on legs when Gran wasn't listening. I can hear the girly giggles just thinking about those days.

He is smiling at me and I'm melting, I really must control myself especially as I am brandishing a sharp knife.

"Hello, is it too early for visiting Kate?"

"Cameron you are welcome anytime you know that," I said with Gran's words of "fast cat" going through my head. "Coffee and toast?" Please say yes, please say yes, I'm thinking.

"Yes please, that will be lovely I do feel a little peckish," he nodded.

"Long day ahead, how is it going?" I'm hopeful for an update.

"Every day and night we are working and I'm afraid we don't have any proper leads so far. It's as though she never existed."

"I was going to speak to Al and Nariman again but it's pretty busy here and with staff shortages I can't go to Leeds yet. What about Lil and the CCTV cameras, any good?"

"Lil didn't know anything more and the cameras are not in operation."

"In other words, broken and I bet they have been like it for a long time." It's typical of Leeds council, looks good but not functioning. "Are you still going with the Spanish possibility?"

"Only because Al saw her looking at the pictures in Miro, that and the fact that there are a lot of Spanish people in Leeds. We asked at the Universities just in case but no luck there either. The hospitals employ a lot of Spanish nurses and healthcare workers, but Al didn't think she spoke much English so not much hope there either." Cameron stopped to eat his toast and drink his coffee.

"I've been thinking Cameron, there are other countries who speak Spanish, she could have been from further away like Ecuador or Colombia."

"Yes, I thought the same but where is her luggage? You don't pop over for a long weekend from places like that."

"No, you don't. Perhaps she lives somewhere else and just came here for a visit." I wish I could think of something good, something more helpful.

I was going to tell him about last night and the horrible attack on Mr Greaves and Flossie. The problem is Mr Greaves doesn't want any interference, it's up to him, I have to respect his wishes. Our time together is usually short lived and true to form Cameron's phone is ringing.

"I'm sorry Kate I have to answer this."

I just nodded and smiled whilst he dealt with the call, that's it, all over, he has to get back. As he stood up to go, still talking on his phone, he stroked me on the shoulder, making my whole body tingle. By the time Cameron had finished his conversation it's obvious something has come to light.

"Can you tell me anything? I mean I can't help but overhear when there's only the two of us, but it sounds like there could be a lead, yes?"

"Perhaps, perhaps not. Drug squad informed us of a drug dealer who has arrived in the area working through parts of Leeds, Harehills and Woodhouse. Hans Dieter, a German dealer who also has his fingers into art theft."

"Sounds promising."

"He drives a black Mercedes."

"That is interesting."

"Time will tell, sorry I have to get back to Leeds, thanks for the coffee and toast."

The faint smell of Imperial Leather soap lingered for a few magical moments after he had gone through the kitchen door, wonderful! My day can now begin, and I wish each morning could start as nicely as this one.

Jennifer and Penelope, Sally's 17-year-old twin nieces have arrived with big warm smiles on their faces, good start. She had forgotten to tell me they are identical twins, very identical in every way, not that it's a big problem. They both know their way around a kitchen alright, a trait which seems to run deep through Sally's large family. Within half an hour they had both donned our spare aprons and were quickly toasting, buttering, and plating up cakes on trays. Why didn't I have them before now? They worked well together and smiled and chatted happily with the customers. Jenny and Penny as they prefer to be called seem to know most of my customers and they appear to know Jenny and Penny apart, a skill I need to work on. Perhaps I can get them to each wear a pink slide or a blue slide in their tied back hair, whilst I learn who is who. I gave Sally a smile, nod and a wink when she looked at me with her eyebrows raised in question, she smiled back reassured.

Miss Hall and Miss Winters have just walked in, excellent the two Wetherby residents who never miss a thing.

"Kate you brave thing tackling that thug last night. Did you see who he was?" Miss Hall leaned forward as she spoke.

"No, unfortunately I didn't see his face I was just so angry and even angrier when he started kicking poor Flossie."

Several tables put down cups, knives and cake forks whilst a noticeable hush descended upon the room.

"Is Flossie alright?" Miss Winters chipped in.

"She is thank you. I think the attacker came off worse than Mr Greaves and Flossie."

"I just happened to be pulling my curtains on when he was about to attack Mr Greaves. Dreadful situation, I really don't know what is happening to Wetherby these days with all this crime," Miss Hall said tutting loudly.

"It's the same everywhere I am afraid Miss Hall. Mr Greaves was just so shocked he didn't want the police, or any fuss made. I hope he is alright, and it doesn't stop him from going out at night." I hoped it would prompt one of them to say something.

"Mr Greaves does like his evenings with 'friends'." This was all Miss Hall said emphasising 'friends'.

Customers began to pile in, all thirsty and wanting cake and a chat. That's what we're here for so it's time to give them what they want. Thank goodness I have the twins today to help out. Not long until closing time and the till has never stopped ringing. Rose would have been in her element had she been here, in person, not ghostly. Flossie has found a little boy to play with her in the garden whilst his mum and grandmother chat with I would imagine a watchful eye on him. Sally has already told them Flossie loves people and he will be safe playing with her, something which always makes my heart swell with pride.

Only another half an hour before closing and still the odd few customers are crossing the threshold. Mr Potter wants to cut the grass tonight when we close, and I really must make a start on my lists. Jenny and Penny have agreed to work when they can through the week and definitely Saturday's. I'm going to give them extra if they will come in on the weekend I'm away in Madrid, fairs fair. Booking the trip is top of one of my lists, that and getting some clothes together. The way things are going I'll just be throwing anything at all into my bag. As they say, "so much to do and so little time to do it in".

Lovely, everyone has now gone it's so peaceful, the only sound is the steady drum of the dishwasher. Mr Potter is coming after he has been to his gardening club which leaves me another hour free. I'm doing well so far as the hotel and flights are now booked for next Friday leaving from Manchester Airport. That should keep Carol and Rose off my back. My haircut is booked for next Tuesday morning, it's all happening! I need to write a list of cakes to bake in advance, produce to buy for Crumbs, so, so much. I'm beginning to realise it's not easy when you have your own business and wondering why on earth I am going at all.

"You are going because you need a break Kitty, that and it was a birthday present from Carol. Don't you think this is a long-awaited gift, 30 years long," Rose said bitterly.

"You're right Rose and I have made a good start on all the planning. It's booked then Carol will pay me back for it all."

"Do tell me you booked first class, sting her for the best!"

"Now, now Rose, anyway how did your ghostly sit in go? Did you get rid of the exorcist?" I'm trying to change the subject which being Rose she will know what and why I am doing it.

"We chased him all the way down the Main Street. He was as white as a sheet and won't be doing any ridiculous rituals for a long time my dear. We partied for ages after, shame we couldn't drink but there you are, it was nice meeting up with old friends and dancing with them."

"Dancing to what?"

"We all sang Ghostbusters of course, hilarious my dear," Rose said triumphantly.

I decided it is best not to comment as she is obviously in a good mood, let happy ghosts lie.

"Right my dear get on with your lists and don't forget to put some ground almonds in with the cherry loaves this time, so much nicer with almond. You're running out of it so double up on the shopping list, oh and ground rice for the tarts."

"How did you know I forgot last time?" Now I'm worrying!

"My dear I may not always be by your side, but I know, oh I know," Rose answered.

Forget the worrying now I'm panicking!

"Mmm" is all I dare say.

"Before I fly, please remember Kitty to keep away from dead bodies and all that."

"Does that include you Rose?" I asked jokingly.

"Kitty I'm your godmother for always and today. There's danger in the air, do be extra careful."

Just as I wanted to clarify that when she says danger in the air it has nothing to do with my impending flight, puff, Rose has flown.

## Chapter Eleven

Flossie and I have been for an early morning walk by the river. It's so peaceful hardly anyone is up and about yet except for the dog walkers and stupid joggers puffing and panting along the path. I couldn't sleep and when I did it was to dream of adding things to my lists. At this rate I will sleep on the train to Manchester and all of the flight to Madrid, not a bad thing as I hate flying.

"Oh, look Flossie, Stan is out bright and early this morning keeping the paths clean."

"Woof."

"Good morning, Stan, are you getting some overtime in?"

"Morning love. Heard all about you and Flossie t'other night. Don't know what is happening in this place with folk attacking innocent folk on the street. Flossie saw him off good and proper though didn't you Flossie lass?" Stan said, bending to give Flossie a scratch under the chin.

"Woof."

"I reckon he'd been waiting for Mr Greaves to come out then attacked him."

"Why do you think that, Stan?"

"Stands to reason lass, him being a bit of a ladies

man. Right as one of them there husbands found out he was playing around with their missus and went to wallop him. The quiet ones are always the worst, and he never says owt at work, ta-ra lass take care," Stan nodded and winked before brushing some litter up and into his dustcart.

"Bye Stan take care," I shouted after him. "Well Flossie let's get home for breakfast and a shower then into the café for all the latest gossip. Wetherby is positively the hotspot for it, who knows what we will find out today."

"Woof."

My three gems are working hard in the kitchen and on the shop floor. The twins actually arrived today wearing slides in their hair, pink ones for Penny (so this old fogey can remember because of p for pink) and blue ones for Jenny, brilliant! Everything is under control, and I have managed to bake two farmhouse fruit cakes and two Madeira cakes plus three trays of buns, long may it last.

Sally has just whispered in my ear that Pippa has arrived with Mr Slimeball on crutches! This I really have to see, not that I wish him ill but let's face it anything that slows down his sliminess has to be a bonus. Yes, there he is with his right ankle all bandaged up the size of a melon. He's hobbling to a table with the metal crutch attached to his arm. Pippa is flapping around him like a mother hen, holding the chair out and taking the crutch from him and propping it up against the wall at the side of him. For better or worse as the wedding vows go and boy will it be worse in his case, mind you mine was no better. How foolish we girls can be when it comes to men.

"Let me have the pleasure of this Sally," I smiled sweetly knowing she would get the message.

"Go ahead be my guest," she said with a mocking bow.

Steering my way through the tables I can see Pippa holding his hand and stroking it gently. Wow he is really milking it, the pig!

"Hello Pippa, oh you've been in the wars, what happened?" I can't bring myself to say his name or even look at him as I speak.

"An accident," Slimeball volunteered.

"Nasty, how did you have an accident? Up a ladder putting light bulbs in for Pippa?" I doubt he would know how or get my sarcasm.

"Poor Antonio was working out in my gym late the other night. I was out with my friend and got a call from the hospital to pick him up. Poor lamb, he's staying with me so I can look after him properly," Pippa pecked him on the cheek and wiped off her red lipstick laughing girlishly.

"I'm sure he will enjoy that." Pass me the sick bucket I want to throw up!

Orders taken, I'm glad to be back in the kitchen away from him. He makes my skin crawl, what the heck is wrong with her? One day she will wake up and find he has wheedled his way into all she has worked hard for and her late husband and family.

Let's hope it doesn't go that far. Sally watched with her eyebrows up, tutting away at them slobbering over each other.

"Sally, can you hold the fort please whilst I dash to the post office? I want to post a card to Al and Nariman to cheer them up."

"Of course, but don't dash, we don't want you sporting Slimeball's other crutch when you are going away next week," Sally winked.

"No chance, thanks I won't be long. Flossie will come with me."

The sky is so blue with just a little breeze and yet the river Wharfe is flowing quite fast. Flossie has dashed off after her friend Dave, a shiny black-haired dachshund. Dog walkers tend to know all the dogs' names but not their owners', unless they are neighbours. Dave's "mum" is a small, round faced cheerful lady who always has a green jacket on with bulging pockets. One pocket is full of Dave's poo bags, empty of course and the other has packets of treats for her dog and any other ones she meets.

"Hello how are you, Kate? Heard all about the other night, brave Flossie, aren't you? Yes, you are, you are," Dave's mum said scratching behind Flossie's ears. Quick as a flash her hand was in the green jacket and pulling out a couple of treats for them both. Flossie is in her doggy 7th heaven.

"News travels fast in Wetherby," I said giving Dave a stroke.

"Sure does, folk around these parts know what

you've done even before it's happened. Take care Kate,"

"I will thank."

As I walked away, I felt goosebumps on my arms even though the sun is warm. Her parting words did not seem the usual automatic meaningless ones people tend to say when leaving each other, strange.

"Good afternoon, Susan, please may I have a first class stamp."

"Hello Kate, you okay?" Susan said passing the stamp over the counter.

"I am thanks, but I wondered if you have seen Mr Greaves and if so, how he is?"

Susan stiffened visibly but then relaxed her shoulders slightly.

"I'm not sure how he is. He must be working but I don't see him socially so how would I know?" she said in a defensive tone.

"Oh, I'm sorry it's because I saw you together, I thought you would have heard from him."

"Well, I haven't."

"Should he come into the post office please give him my best wishes."

Susan coloured up and put her head down.

"Goodbye," I said trying to sound cheerful but inside I'm feeling pretty miffed at her attitude. Chocolate! I need chocolate, to heck with cutting back for Madrid it's the cure for all moods and situations. "Come on Flossie just one more shop then we have to get back to Crumbs. I hope the customers are all in better moods than Susan."

"Woof."

The nearest newsagents is in the town square and they have a wonderful selection of chocolate bars and sweets, my kind of shop. I'm like a kid when faced with them all, it takes me ages to decide. Greasy Lorraine has run the shop since before Rose bought Crumbs café and she has always looked the same. I don't wish to be unkind, but she just looks greasy. Lorraine's long brown hair is parted down the middle and usually put behind her ears, just hanging there limply, greasily. Her face and hands always look incredibly grubby, as though all the print from the newspapers has wiped off onto them. She has put weight on, particularly around her chest area which she tends to rest on the counter when she sits on her chair. They must weigh a heck of a lot if she can't support them herself, not comfortable and certainly not a pleasant sight. There she is behind the counter or should I say "on" the counter.

"Hello Lorraine"

"Na then Kate," she grunted as she flicked through a magazine without looking up.

I don't know why I look at all the different chocolate bars because I always end up with the same one in the end, force of habit. Holding out my Snickers bar and money, the overhead light is highlighting the grease on Lorraine's face and hair. If the chocolate bar were not covered, I don't think

I could have bought it after looking at Lorraine's face and hair.

"What yer reckon to Madam Muck and that Spaniard tying the knot then?" she asked taking my money.

The whole transaction was done without getting up from her chair. Money taken, put into the till at the side of her and change given back, chest still on its perch. No wonder she has put weight on, she has everything at her greasy fingertips.

"Pippa has got engaged but I don't think she is ready to marry him yet."

"Ee's the clutching type, knows ee's on to a good thing that one, she must be soft in the head. Weddings 'appening in a few weeks."

"No!"

"That's what our Frieda says to me no more than an hour ago and she got it from 'er mate who works for Madame Muck."

"I can't understand it, they were in Crumbs and never said anything." Mind you I didn't give Pippa much opportunity to.

"There's no fool like an old fool," Greasy Lorraine said shoving half a packet of crisps into her mouth and licking the salt and vinegar flavouring off her fingers.

"Come on Flossie let's go." Before I'm physically sick!

"Woof."

Sally couldn't believe the news of the wedding. Although we are busy Lorraine's words keep coming back to me about old fools. Gran used to say the same and it has really unsettled me, Pippa could do better, she's so nice.

"Why don't you have a word with her Kate? It's eating away at you."

"And say what? Don't marry him because he's a slimeball, that would really change her mind."

"Well just talk to her about her plans. Find out how, when, and where and at least you know more then, and it gives you time to think it through. You can't deny you would do something about it if it really was bad for her," Sally said holding my hand.

"You forgot the why and you are right as usual, I would do something."

Jenny and Penny are free to work more next week and the weekend I'm in Madrid. If I am super organised with shopping, baking, packing then I should be ready to leave next Friday afternoon. So much is happening now that I wish I had not gone ahead with the booking just yet. I should be looking forward to it but honestly, I'm not. Mr Potter will take Flossie home with him on an evening and be there to assist and walk her during the day, there's too much to think of.

The sun brings the coach parties which for all of the businesses around Wetherby is good. Lots stop off either en route to Harrogate or further up North. When the sun shines the tills ring. I've managed to get hold of Pippa this lunchtime in between customers and takeaway orders. She's very busy her end but has asked me to meet her at her hotel for a drink this evening. If Slimeball is there it will not be so easy, but it may be my only chance to discuss her plans.

"What do you think Flossie to this dress, not bad is it? Flossie, I have to make an effort if I'm going to the Davenport Manor Hotel for drinks plus if he's there I don't know, I'm hoping it gives me more confidence."

"Woof."

"Just let me get my pashmina and we're ready for off." Opening my scarf draw everything is rolled and colour placed, something which amazes me as the rest of my drawers are a total mess. If ever I had burglars, they would think someone had got there before them, particularly my knicker drawer, shameful.

As I'm pulling out a pretty floral-patterned pashmina in shades of blue and pink to go with my light blue linen dress it's jolted me back to finding the murder victim's blue one in Miro. Goosebumps are covering my arms and a cold shiver is running down my back, poor soul, who is she?

"Jump in Flossie let's get this over with."

Flossie is looking at me with one ear up and the other flat with her head on one side. I wish I knew what she is thinking.

The Davenport Manor Hotel is buzzing with

guests and people booking into the spa. I hope we can find somewhere quiet to sit and talk. Flossie is walking very close to my heels and enjoying the friendly patting from some of the guests.

"Hello Kate."

Walking towards me with a broad smile that's lighting up his eyes is Cameron. Am I glad I made an effort! His face is telling me how much he approves of what he sees.

"Hello Cameron. Pippa invited me for a drink and Flossie of course."

"Of course," he said bending to have a cuddle with Flossie. "You look amazing Kate; I mean you always look nice, but I've never seen you dressed before."

An elderly lady walking past looked at him, then me, winked and said, "Go girl!" I blushed to the roots of my soon to be cut hair. Cameron laughed.

"Sorry for that but you know what I mean."

"I do," I answered. "Are you here in an official capacity, may I ask or is it none of my business?"

Cameron made a tutting sound as he pulled a face. "Just updating her because of her texts and before you ask no, we are no further to finding out who the sender of them is."

"So, it's still happening."

"It is, something I'm sure she will discuss with you."

"Oh, I'm sorry about that. I'm hoping to find out more about the wedding plans. I've only just been told they are going ahead soon, something she neglected to tell me about in Crumbs yesterday."

"Perhaps she didn't know then, but it does all seem very rushed."

"I'll let you know what I find out in case it has any bearing on the texts."

"Thank you, goodnight."

Oh, why can't I be here having drinks with him instead? Perhaps when all this mad rush of going to Madrid is over. How I wish it could be postponed, better still cancelled.

Pippa looks amazing, she is positively glowing from head to foot. It's hard to imagine her ever looking like she has been pulled through a hedge backwards as I do first thing in the morning. Why can't I have style like her? Wearing a simple dreamy black dress which floated around the hemline as she walked towards me, red shoes and accessories all to go with the new ruby and diamond ring no doubt. You cannot get away from it, this lady is classy.

Thankfully as yet there is no sign of Slimeball, he may make an appearance later after she has paved the way. We are in a cosy corner of the library, all beautiful wood and wall to wall shelving packed with books old and new. The floor is highly polished with a circular rug in warm colours, leather high backed armchairs in dark green and two small mahogany tables.

"Please be comfortable Kate, what would you like to drink?"

"Just orange juice please with ice, I'm driving.

Is Flossie alright in here? It's so lovely," I asked feeling guilty for bringing her.

"She certainly is."

"I won't be a moment," Pippa smiled her radiant smile and floated to the bar area.

"Look at this room Flossie, it's wonderful. Books from all over the world and those up there must be very old. Leather bound and gold embossing. I'm in a very special room."

"Woof," Flossie barked gently moving her head from side to side looking up and down the bookshelves.

"Here we are," Pippa glided gracefully through the door with a silver tray holding a glass of white wine and a glass of orange juice, a silver dish of nibbles and something in a small bag. "This is for you Flossie. I'm sorry, she can have it can't she Kate? It's only some small doggy treats."

"You try and stop her Pippa; you're very kind thank you."

Flossie sat obediently, her tail sweeping the floor until Pippa opened the bag and gave her a few. How to win my dog over in one easy lesson!

"So is Antonio joining us tonight?" This way I will know how much I can say and indeed ask.

"He thought it would be nice for us to have a girls night only. I have some news to tell you," Pippa said sipping her white wine.

More like he didn't want to be interrogated, the coward.

"That's a shame I could have asked him about

Madrid. Is he feeling better?" I don't really care but I have to stay nice, "two faced" Gran would have said. So what! He's a slimeball.

"Much better thank you. He's back at the hospital on Tuesday for a check-up then if it's stronger he will be in London on Friday for a few days of meetings with business associates."

"At least he can get stronger by swimming in your pool." I have to pretend to be slightly sympathetic for Pippa's sake.

"Oh no, he can't swim. I know it's crazy, isn't it? A Spaniard who can't swim. Apparently, he grew up on a farm with very little money so never had the chance for holidays by the beach," Pippa said shaking her head.

I couldn't care less because I don't know if I could believe a thing he says. Something niggles me all the time and it's nothing to do with our auras clashing.

"Antonio's always working so hard on either the phone or his laptop. You know yourself how hard it is when you run your own business, all work and very little play."

My heart bleeds for him!

"Still, we will get a break for our honeymoon soon, in four weeks," Pippa paused looking at me with a slightly flushed face. "I know what you're thinking Kate."

No, you really don't!

"It's too soon, I haven't known him long, do I really know him? Why rush?"

I take it back she does know what I'm thinking, that and much more.

"He asked me when we got back here after Crumbs yesterday. I can honestly tell you I wasn't expecting the wedding date so soon but then I didn't expect the beautiful engagement ring either." She held out her hand and the diamonds burst into sparkling colours with the lamp's glow.

"We're getting married here, well I suppose it makes sense, then flying to Spain to tour around and meet what's left of his family. Before we come back, I will get to see his restaurant, meet his staff, check everything out for myself, get the whole picture."

"The whole picture, what do you mean by that?" I'm trying to sound reasonable but inside my guts feel twisted, psychic or intuition?

"We are going to be partners in more than just marriage Kate. I'm investing in the restaurant; we will be expanding into the wedding trade big time. The restaurant is next to the palace gardens and a big church, so it makes good business sense to capitalise on weddings, christenings etc."

"Antonio has got it all worked out." I'm speechless and very aware my face is telling how I really feel. Action Kate, get out of this with your friendship still intact, she will need it! I'm raising my glass of orange juice to toast them.

"To true partnership." Let her read into that what she may. Our glasses are clinking but I will find it hard to swallow, all of it.

# Chapter Twelve

"Kate, stop fidgeting I'm only giving you a trim not decapitating you," Tracy is gently pushing down on my gown covered shoulders.

"Sorry you know how I get; I just hate sitting and not being in control of what's happening." I'm not comfortable in hairdressing salons, especially when they don't do what you ask for.

"Watch in the mirror and shout at me if I'm not doing what you want," Tracy smirked knowingly.

"You must be joking! How can I shout at someone who is holding a pair of sharp scissors close to my neck? Do you think I want to be the next victim, again?"

"Right then, do as you are told, sit up straight and let's make you look like a film star for Madrid," Tracy said tightening the crossover fastening of the salon's gown.

"Steady," I said joking "I've had this done to me recently!"

Just as she is starting to comb through my hair the young girl on reception is calling to her. A client on the phone needs to discuss colours, something the receptionist hasn't a clue about. Looking at her it's fair to say she may not have a clue about anything unless it's to do with her social media account. Tracy excused herself.

My attention is suddenly drawn to two females sitting with towels on their shoulders and tin foil sticking out at different angles around their crowning glories. It made me think of Christmas turkeys.

"What do you think of that divine hunk Pippa has managed to hook?" Tin Foil One is saying to Tin Foil Two.

"Hunk with a capital H! He smells divine too, I'd wash his socks any day," Tin Foil Two replied.

"Fun for a while. As long as she can cope with his roving eyes, and hands then good luck to her," Tin Foil One has added.

"No!"

"Yes, defo yes, I've been on the receiving end at that get together last week in her hotel, the library no less. Fun for two minutes then reality hit home," Tin Foil One admitted.

"Have you no shame sweetie?" Tin Foil Two asked.

"Let me think on that for a minute," Tin Foil One said looking demure. "No."

Both Tin Foils burst into controlled laughter obviously due to the amounts of Botox and fillers controlling their faces. All very interesting but a little disturbing to say the least.

My hair looks great, but I feel totally rubbish. At the moment I don't think anything will manage to cheer me up. Why is it everything comes at once?

Time is racing now, could I postpone this trip? Nothing feels right somehow, I feel I will be needed more at home.

Sally has a silly grin on her face every time she passes me.

"What's with the grin?"

"You don't know how many people have commented today on your new look. "Quite the stunner" old Mr Jenkins said which got him a slap from Mrs Jenkins. It really suits you shorter so smile a bit more, what's going on it's not like you?" Sally asked.

"Have you time for a coffee when we close? I could do with your opinion on something."

"Ten minutes is neither here nor there when the kids are being looked after by their grandmother," Sally said kindly.

"Thanks, if it turns quiet, we can close a little earlier."

It turned out to be a quiet last hour, so someone is working on my side, as long as they don't do it again and spoil my trading. Sally is listening to everything, that's one of her qualities she listens without interrupting. She took a moment to digest it all, sipping her coffee looking straight at me hands on the table fingers spread out like a fan.

"You have to find out more about him Kate, he's a con I'm sure of it. Pippa is a lovely person who deserves better than that."

"My thoughts exactly Sally. So much is happening, and I don't feel good or easy about any of it. The stupid trip is wrong, the timing is wrong, and I really regret booking it. Should I cancel?"

"No, you should not! You need a break and there's not much you could do here in these three days except keep your ears open. The girls, Mr Potter and I, we can do that and Flossie of course," Sally bent down to stroke Flossie as she spoke. Flossie responded by standing up with her ears twitching back and forth.

"Woof."

"There you are Flossie, welcome to the Spy Team," Sally laughed.

"You're right I know, but..."

"No buts, you are going. Spend your time on the train and plane thinking how you can approach Pippa with whatever we find out. When you get to Madrid forget it all and relax, that's an order."

"Yes ma'am, thanks ma'am." I'm smiling, grateful to have such a good friend around for me.


Al and Nariman have left a voicemail thanking me for the card I had sent them. They don't know anything new about the murder and wish me a good trip. The way the hours are flying past there will be little chance of me visiting them, they wouldn't expect me to, but it would be nice.

The freezer is now groaning it's so full of baked items and by Thursday the fridge will be the same, just in case. My body feels totally charged. Perhaps I'm one of those people who operates better with little sleep and lots of stress, it won't last, it can't. It's 9:15 PM and the TV options are unbelievably mind bogglingly boring.

"Fancy a walk, Flossie?"

"Woof."

The air is warm and filled with the heavy scent of roses as we walk past gardens full of them, Rose would have loved them. I'm not keen on yellow ones myself although some yellow roses have a fresh lemony perfume which is nice. This is so peaceful, Wetherby feels relaxed and sleepy tonight, maybe people are sitting in their gardens with friends and family. That's something I hope to do one day when Mr Right comes along.

Flossie who has quite a length out on her lead has stopped dead on the corner leading to the cottages. Her left front paw is paused in mid-air and her ears are twitching, time to quicken my pace.

"What's going on Flossie? Is someone out there?" I'm whispering in case the night air carries my voice. "Ah I see now." outside Mr Greaves' cottage is Susan Walsh and she's crying. Actually, the way her shoulders are moving she's sobbing. Mr Greaves is walking down the steps and putting his arm around her. His head is very close to hers, does this mean she is one of his ladies as well? She could have found out about the others, maybe even walked in on one of them in the cottage, wow, poor Susan. All must be forgiven now though as she is leaning against him, ah, that's nice. Now do I walk on or retrace my steps? Retrace, it's less embarrassing for all concerned.

My holdall is packed except for my makeup bag which I'm still using, and my handbag will need checking for everything on Friday morning. For me this is pretty well organised even if I say so myself, I have to as there's nobody else to say it for me. Tomorrow is left for shopping for the fridge- fruit, cream, butter. Milk is delivered to Crumbs daily so that's fine. Teas and coffees are well stocked as all the serviettes and paper tray covers. Honestly this is like planning for Christmas. The lists are almost all ticked off.

Pippa has just breezed in looking like a ray of sunshine in a summery yellow dress printed with small white daisies, cute and classy as always.

"Good afternoon, Pippa what can I get you or are you waiting for Antonio?"

"No, it's only me Kate, I've just taken him to the railway station in Leeds, he's gone to London earlier than expected. I'm feeling a bit old without him, so I came here instead of straight back to the Manor."

"Oh, you know it's always good to see you, is his foot better or has he still got to use the crutch?" I can hope, can't I?

"Less bandage but still with the crutch poor

love. He says he will manage as it's mostly sitting in all the meetings around London. He can get taxis to wherever he needs to go so bless him he will keep going." Pippa smiled a lovesick smile.

Me, I'd like to knock his crutch from under him if I came face to face with him in the street. I've had my fill of liars and cheats.

"Come into the kitchen whilst I make your coffee, and do you want any farmhouse fruit cake?"

"I really should be watching what I eat for the dress fitting next week but your cake is always irresistible. Go on then just a small portion please."

"So, you have moved on with the wedding plans." I tried not to sound dismayed but it's so hard.

"Just a few more things to book like flowers and the printing of the invitations. Antonio is leaving it all to me as he is down South, that's meant for you. As long as I am happy then so is he."

I bet, the slimeball! What's the betting Pippa is paying for everything and he will "sort it out later", pigs will fly! I really don't want to burst her bubble but the feeling inside of me whenever he is mentioned is getting worse. As Sally said I can assess it on the plane which will probably involve me writing a list of what I know so far. Lists bring clarity to my complex situations.

"Are you excited about your trip to Madrid?" Pippa asked.

"Yes and no would be the honest answer, I'm too

tired and part of me feels guilty for leaving the girls and Mr Potter." I can't say all the truth it's not easy to do that to my friend, so I've given her some of it.

"When you get to the airport and then on the plane you will be excited. I can't wait to fly there with my new husband, the hotel will be in good hands whilst we have some fun in the sun" she grinned.

Oh my word! That's yuck with a capital Y. Things could change by then, he could do the decent thing and run off with someone else, not nice for Pippa but better in the end.

"Anyway, what time do you get back into Leeds railway station on Monday? Only I'm at my dress fitting in needs and if it ties in, I could pick you up."

There's no way I could share the car all the way from Leeds to Wetherby with Slimeball slobbering all over her. I need to ask gently.

"What time does Antonio get in? I don't want you hanging around for me."

"Bless you Kate but no, Antonio is away all next week and I'm planning a good shopping trip on Monday afternoon. Some retail therapy in the Harvey Nichols store is what I need to cheer me up, and the chance to buy something special for my groom. We could meet for coffee in the Queens Hotel, that way I can just relax until your train arrives."

"My train gets in around 4:30 PM on Monday so that would be perfect. Thank you Pippa I will look forward to that. Here you are, tell me what you think to the new recipe, well my changes to Gran's old recipe."

"Delicious, light, fruity with a hint of Christmas spices. If you want to bake for the Davenport Hotel, just say the word."

"A little bit more?" not that I'm trying to force feed her, more like trying to give her some good old home comforting.

"No, no, oh go on then why not?" Pippa laughed holding out her plate.

"Take it out into the garden with Flossie but don't give into her pleading eyes. Watch out, she will try all the tricks in the book so be strong." Just like Slimeball I wanted to say but can't. Flossie has a cross look on her face because of what I have just said but like Pippa she will ignore it, in time.

## Chapter Thirteen

Phone charger! There I am congratulating myself but the one major thing apart from my passport not on my list is my phone charger. If I put it on top of my holdall, I can charge up my phone tonight and then slip it straight into my bag.

Sally and the girls have taken control of Crumbs whilst I do the last-minute shopping with Flossie. That will be the end of it and my lists will be all ticked off.

"Come on girl let's get some good old English fish and chips, fancy a bite?"

"Woof."

There's a bit of a queue but the staff know how to work through it quickly. Four from the front is a head I would recognise anywhere. The dark well-cut hair is growing into adorable little "kiss curls" around the collar area. How I could just tease them around my finger, oooh stop it, Kate!

"Cameron!" I'm trying to call in a ladylike fashion. Rose will approve. The dark head has turned, and Cameron's face is lit up with a gorgeous smile.

"Hello, I'm saving your place Kate," he replied

beckoning to me. A bit confusing but I think he's pretending so I'll follow his lead.

"Thanks Cameron," melting inside as he winks at me.

"Shall we take them to the river? I'll get yours and a little extra for Flossie," he said happily.

The sun is glistening on the water, birds are busy singing their mating songs, ducks and drakes swimming together and I'm sitting next to a handsome man as I lick salt and vinegar off my fingers! Not very ladylike now, but so, so good.

"This is very peaceful, thank you for our lunch."

Flossie is tucking into a large sausage, also naughty but nice.

"You are very welcome. It's lovely to have a break with you, sorry I haven't had much time recently. You fly tomorrow, have a lovely trip, won't you?"

"I'll try." Dare I say it? Yes, he can only say yes or no. "Have dinner with me when I get back so I can tell you how it went, the short version, promise."

"Can't wait, whichever version you want to give," this voice held sincerity.

Stupid idiot that I am, I'm blushing like a schoolgirl. "Can I ask if there's any news?"

"You can but all I can say is the truth, which is we are pursuing all avenues, not getting far but we haven't much to go on."

I told him about Pippa's plans and my fears, he stayed quiet and thoughtful looking. I also told him what the Tin Foils had said.

"When a friend cannot see or want to see the truth, it's hard to step back. Let it go for a little longer. Unless you get more proof there is not much else you can do without risking your friendship. I'm here if you need support in anyway." He leaned against me and briefly held my hand; I swear I won't wash it again. He makes me feel like a teenager!

Lunch break was over far too soon, work beckoned for both of us. Cameron was able to walk halfway back to Crumbs with us and give me a goodbye hug. For a few moments I felt he would kiss me, maybe next time.

Tomorrow night I will be in a strange bed in a strange place. Tonight, I'm happily snuggling down under my duvet with all my familiar things and smells around me, safe, homely and content. Flossie is in her bed on the landing, on guard with one ear cocked and her gentle snores drifting through my half open bedroom door. I can see the clothes I am going to travel in over the back of my Gran's chair that she used in her own bedroom. Her gentle singing of "Christopher Robin is saying his prayers" is going around my head. Goodnight Gran and Rose, love you.

Manchester Airport is buzzing, a real people watcher's heaven. Imagining where passengers are going, what for and better still are they with their true partners or bits on the side? This is what gets me through the torture of the actual flight, which I hate. Sometimes my toilet trips before boarding can lift the heads of those more relaxed passengers watching me, tough! I'm through security now and walking into the shopping area with cafés and bars. These are the final stages before the snaking queues, not much time left now. I've only got my bag so it will be nice to have some distraction for a short time. Champagne and oysters, wow that's going a bit far before flying. Hope it doesn't get rough up there, I don't fancy a passenger bringing up what they just paid the earth for all down the back of my seat. Madness, pure madness all for love, that or to impress her.

Oh my goodness! I don't believe what my eyes have just clocked onto. SLIMEBALL! No bandaged foot, no crutch, clinking champagne flutes together with a female. A flame haired, red fingernailed female with eyes only for him. They're kissing and offering each other an oyster, suggestive looks and talk followed by laughter, I hope he chokes on it! Judging by her clothes and shoes (red soles) and handbag, she has loads of money. They must be flying away together otherwise they wouldn't be in this part of the airport. I knew it, I can smell a rat a mile away now. I've got to stay calm, keep my distance and watch them. Photo, that's it if I can get a photo for proof. That's what Cameron was talking about, the need for proof. I'll figure out what to do with it later.

"Can I help you Madame?" a voice behind me is

asking.

Spinning around and almost knocking over a stand with leather purses on it, I'm facing a rather stern looking female shop assistant. What can I say? If I don't act fast, I won't get a photo of them from a safe place. OK here goes, keep to the semi truth.

"How do you feel about two timing, cheating slimeballs ruining the lives of genuinely nice ladies, perhaps on multiple occasions?" My eyes are wide open appealing to her, fingers crossed behind my back.

"That one there drinking champagne and guzzling oysters with the redhead?" She pointed between the stands of scarves.

"Yes, I need a photo for proof."

"Then take it with my pleasure. Get him where it hurts, his wallet. That's what he's after. He's a total creepy toad that one. I see them all the time sitting there, spinning their charm and lies," she said stepping aside.

I took six photos, mostly of them kissing, cuddling and drinking. Got you, you umpteen timing Slimeball. There's no squirming out of this one Antonio.

"Thank you. I just hope I can get through to the lady he is marrying in three weeks' time without damaging her trust and our friendship."

"You will, good luck," she held my arm gently. "Just be careful there is danger around that one, he has a dark aura," she said turning and walking away to serve another customer.

Dark auras? Danger? There is that word again and this time it's not Rose telling me. Toilet, I need to go now, I'm feeling desperate for the loo. I know I'm stupid and it's nerves because I will be boarding soon but I must go, now!

Before I have to switch my phone off, I need to tell Sally what I have seen and make sure she keeps her eyes and ears open for any snippets from the ladies or Mr Greaves.

My eyes are firmly closed, and my knuckles are white with gripping the seat's armrests, I absolutely detest flying. The one good thing about this flight is it's only half full and Slimeball and the redhead are not amongst the few passengers on board. My head was on swivel mode as I queued up to board, the security cameras must have been suspicious. Okay we're up! If I had a normal existence in a normal business situation taking a well-earned break, I would say being up in the air I feel closer to Rose. That's not the case for me, she can pop in and out of my café and my life at any moment, or the seat next to me. I'll think about the landing part nearer the time.

Nobody is sitting in the other two seats next to me so no distractions whilst I think through Pippa's heart-breaking situation. Paper and pen at the ready to write down all I know, have heard or seen; it's how I can fathom things out. Ah coffee is being brought by the stewardess, that will recharge my mind.

"Thank you, no sugar just milk please." Now to work.

An hour has literally flown by. My written thoughts, observations, overheard snippets of conversations have covered more pages than I expected. In all the recent events which have happened around Wetherby there is one common denominator, Slimeball. I don't have the evidence but the looks, odd word said, fear on some faces, reactions when he is around, it's there. I know it is, I will find it.

Not long to go before landing and my plan of action has been formulated. Pippa gave me an indication of where his restaurant is, and I'm going to visit it, why not! As it is next to the King of Spain's old hunting lodge palace and beautiful palace gardens, it can't be hard to find.

"Promises, promises. Kitty yours are like cheap washing up liquid, they fizzle out."

"Rose, how on earth did you get here?" Immediately as the words are out, I know that's such a stupid question to ask her. I'm just shocked she's next to me, on an aeroplane.

"Faster than you my dear but don't worry I won't stop with you for long. I wanted to make sure you are alright and much to my dismay I find you are plotting away instead of relaxing."

"If you know all that then you will know why I am doing it. Did you see him in the airport? Come on Rose you know more so how about joining forces and helping me?"

At this point I can see the passengers the other side of the aisle staring across at me. I admit it must look and sound strange with me talking to the back of the seat in front of me. I have to redeem myself quickly before they call security to check me out or whatever they do. So, turning to them all with a smile, here goes.

"Oh, I'm sorry I disturbed you all, I'm a writer and I'm so used to talking through some of my scenes at home." There I think that's pretty quick thinking and going by the smiles and waves it has worked.

Rose is chuckling away next to me but what I need is for her to fly off out of here. I paid, well technically Carol did but Rose is a stowaway. Time for that thought transfer malarkey, here goes, eyes closed.

"Rose, can you hear me?"

"Stop shouting Kitty my dear, I'm dead not deaf."

"Sorry. Is there anything you can do please?"

"As I have said before Kitty, I will always protect you. Please stop all this and concentrate on enjoying your weekend."

"I can't stop it, but I will be careful. I'm going there to see for myself where his money is invested and how good the restaurant really is."

"Talking of seeing, they have cameras in the loos on this plane my dear. Security is high and the screens are in the cockpit monitoring nearly everything," Rose chuckled.

"No!"

"Yes, from the waist up for modesty. Not all airlines are the same so go steady on the drinks Kitty, bye bye my dear."

Suddenly my silence was not so golden, and I had gone off my coffee.

Landing at Madrid confirmed my dread of flying. Our captain who sounded so dishy over the plane's airwaves had introduced himself as Captain Bird. No matter how it is spelt he cannot fly like one! The plane did kangaroo jumps down the runway until it stopped on a 10 pence piece and my head almost shot through the seat in front, I hate flying and now I have the marks on my forehead to prove it.

Carol has come up trumps with this birthday present. The sun is shining, to be expected I suppose it's not exactly Bridlington. Hotel Emperador is impressive and luxurious, I love it. Lunch is taken later here so when in Spain... When I have eaten, I will consult my list of places to visit and stroll around, sit, drink and people watch. I can feel some of the tension leaving my body already.

Madrid is so beautiful. Its architecture, shops, food (thanks to Rose and her friends' recommendations) so far so good. As for taking advantage of the ultra warm evening air and the bars, I'm too exhausted. It's been such a long draining day. All the worry and rushing around is finally catching up with me. Tomorrow I will come back early to explore the shops on Gran Vía properly then return to Plaza Mayor for a Spanish lunch. If I have the energy there are museums, the Retiro park, the Prado, my list is too long for two days. Cameron's face floated into my head, perhaps, who knows what may happen in the future, we could come back together.

I must have still been smiling as I walked through the hotel's lobby, enough to catch the eye of the lovely older receptionist not surprisingly still on duty at nearly 9:00 PM.

"Ah señora looks very happy. Are you now in love with Madrid or have you met someone to make you in love?" She smiled a motherly smile.

"Perhaps both, time will tell. Please may I ask if it is possible to have something light to eat sent to my room? It's been a long day."

"Of course, you may. Would you like a menu to choose whatever you feel like from? You can relax in your bath and then it will be delivered to your room when you are ready to eat."

"Thank you I can cope with that," I said grateful she understands.

"Tomorrow is another day."

Shocked I glanced at her badge which says her name is Rosa, surely a coincidence.

"Yes, you are so right, my Gran and my godmother Rose always said that to me."

"And we know best," she smiled again.

As I look through the hotel's extensive menu,

Rosa is dealing with one enquiry after another, some sound rude. Obnoxious guests sound the same in any language. Suddenly my nostrils are doing a Flossie, ooh I miss her! They're twitching and it's getting stronger. A very well-dressed gentleman in his late 50s, dark hair greying at the sides, gold watch which screams money, is asking for directions. Something about him is jogging my memory but I'm not sure what. It must be smell otherwise why would my nose twitch so much? He's gone now. Rosa has caught me sniffing the air, well it's not an act easily disguised especially with my sound effects.

"Have you decided on your order señora?"

"Yes, I have thank you." I pointed to the menu as it seems an easier option as my Spanish is rubbish. "Could I ask you something else please Rosa?"

"I am here to help you."

"It may sound strange but the gentleman standing next to me just a moment ago," I notice her eyebrows go up. I know what she is thinking, that I'm an escort or worse! "No, no, it's just I have smelled his aftershave before or at least I think I have, do you recognise it and know the name please?" I could be wrong, it's something I need to think more about when I'm not so tired.

"It was strong, wasn't it? The gentleman was wearing one called "Brummel" a very old brand we have had for so many years. Have you been to Spain before?"

"About twelve years ago as a teenager with a

group of friends," I recalled.

"It was very popular then, still is but usually with gentlemen who are a little older."

"Thank you, I have plenty of time for a soak in the bath so could I have my order in 45 minutes please? That will be wonderful."

"Have a good evening señora."

"You too, goodnight."

## Chapter Fourteen

Gosh, I can't remember the last time I slept so well, the pillows, mattress and duvet are as plump and soft as fluffy clouds in the sky, well English skies. This morning is a clear blue sky and it's going to be quite hot. My plans for today were totally rearranged by the time I had got out of the bath last night and into the thick white towelling bathrobe folded on the towel rack. Why don't I have one like this at home? All this has made me realise what I have done without or put up with over the last few years, this worm will turn!

Today I will go around the shops this morning whilst it is not so hot then catch the train to Aranjuez and find Antonio's restaurant. If it is next to the palace gardens it will be easy to find and give me a bit of sightseeing at the same time. I lathered myself in factor 50 which will be needed by this lunchtime as we're in for scorcher today, shame as to me it's defeating the lovely shower and posh smelling shower gel I used. Breakfast next then out into new beautiful places to explore.

Shops are shops to me no matter where you are, perhaps I have got out of doing all of that, or just got older. That's a very sobering thought. The train was very straight forward so I am feeling quite proud of myself standing outside La Almazara restaurant. It's actually bigger than I imagined and very busy with local families having their extended lunches. Let's hope they're not too busy to talk to me, here goes.

"Good afternoon, do you speak English please?" I'm asking the efficient lady on the desk in the entrance.

"Yes, a little," the lady answered without smiling.

"Please may I speak with the manager?" I'm trying to speak slowly but not loudly as so many English people tend to do when talking to foreigners.

One over plucked black eyebrow shot up whilst her thin red lipsticked mouth narrowed. She's glaring at me intently. Any moment she could point her fingers at me and "puff" I'm up in red hot flames. This is so awkward, if only I spoke more Spanish, enough to get me through ordeals like this. Smile Kate, just melt her ice-cold stare with a big stupid grin. She has turned and marched down the room past the bar and into a door marked "Privado". Phew!

Well, business is booming today in the dining room and on the terrace, maybe I was wrong to judge so soon. There's a lot of loud talking amongst the diners, something I noticed in Madrid as well. They're definitely not arguing as ever so often they burst into hearty laughter. It reminds me of the time we went to Butlins holiday camp when I was little and the food hall was packed and noisy, frightening for a young child, all loud voices and the clatter of cutlery.

"Hello, I am Señor Rodriguez. How can I help you señora?" a velvety voice broke through my thoughts. I'm looking up into a tanned face framed by black hair and the deepest dark brown eyes I've ever seen, even deeper than Cameron's. His light blue suit and brilliant white shirt just scream of class and money.

"I'm sorry to interrupt you at your busy time. I'm on a short trip here and as my friend is marrying the owner of this restaurant in a few weeks' time I thought I would come for lunch. I've heard so much about it from my friend in England."

His face looks totally confused, not the reaction I expected.

"Marrying in a few weeks? Please do not tell my wife I'm getting married; my life will be over!" he said running his finger around his neck like a knife cutting his throat.

Now I'm confused.

"Let me show you to a seat, we will have a coffee and you can tell me more," he said walking to a quieter corner of the room.

The coffee is excellent, note to self to get the brand name. I suddenly feel so foolish, but this has to be explained.

"Señor Rodriguez, my friend is marrying

Antonio Lopez in England and also investing in this business."

"And understandably you happened to be here and want to protect your friend and her investment. You are very wise señora. I am the owner and have been for many years. The name Antonio Lopez means nothing to me."

I feel so sick! What the heck am I going to do now?

"Señora…señora, Are you alright?"

"No not really," my head is swimming, please don't let me faint.

Señor Rodriguez clicked his fingers and a young waiter appeared at our table. He said something in Spanish and the young man rushed off returning in seconds with iced water and small dishes of tapas.

"Please try to eat something you will feel better," he said pushing the dishes closer.

The food is truly delicious, and he was right I do feel better for eating and drinking the water.

"Do you have a description of this Antonio Lopez?" he asked kindly.

I suddenly remembered the six photos from the airport. My heart sank as I got my phone from my bag and showed him a photo.

"Ah, your friend is very pretty."

"That's not my friend." Right now, I feel like a private investigator working a divorce case, dirty business divorce cases. He's looking at me and nodding.

"Oh yes, I know him and you're the second lady in the past few months to come looking for him. His name is Carlos Romero. I finished him three years ago for his problems with money and women. He was stealing both money from me and preying on wealthy women."

This is far worse than I could ever have imagined. Slimeball is a big con man, I knew he was a bad one I felt it deeply. Something tells me it hasn't finished at that.

"One moment please and I will call one of my waiters over. He worked with him, and they shared an apartment together for a short time."

Señor Rodriguez waved to an older waiter and beckoned him to our table. They are speaking in Spanish so fast I would never have been able to keep up with them even if I could speak the language fluently. The waiter has turned to me with a sad look on his face.

"Señora I am sorry for your friend but also happy you can save her from the monster. He is not a good man, lots of women, lots of lies. He promises to marry them and then takes their money." The waiter looked towards his boss, who nodded. "I think his wife came looking for him a few months ago."

"His wife?" I feel like I am choking on the words.

"He once said something about his wife. He left her because she was not normal."

"What did he mean by that? Is she suffering in some way medically?"

"He never said but the way he spoke I think something was wrong. He said she threw things, shouted but to me that is part of any marriage." He's smiling at Señor Rodriguez. "She was nice, just very upset." He seems embarrassed by what he has just said. "I went to get Señor Rodriguez, but she had gone when we got back."

"Thank you." What else can I say? It's not their problem anymore. It's mine, a big problem.

Finishing my food is feeling difficult but as the hospitality and kindness shown to me is faultless, I'm forcing it down. I need to get out of here quickly. What I really want is to be back in Wetherby, amongst my friends. With thanks, handshakes and contact details given, Cameron will need contact with them, I've walked out into the heat. Heat, shock and sickness in my stomach are all whizzing around me like clothes spinning in the washing machine. I have lost any interest I had in exploring the palace gardens. It's the train and back to the hotel for me.

To be perfectly honest, how I feel after what I have learnt in Aranjuez is nothing compared to how I am going to feel dealing with it. My good instincts do not usually fail me. There are the few exceptions of course, meaning one big one, Matt the Rat, but we all learn something from failure. I've had time to reflect on the last few weeks leading up to this discovery. I have thought carefully and made another list on the train journey back to Madrid. I need to contact Sally and Cameron later from my hotel bedroom, after a large stiff drink, or two.

Thank goodness Rosa's friendly face is greeting me at reception. I can feel tears pricking my eyes and at the moment they are dangerously close to flowing freely down my cheeks.

"Señora...you have not had a good day?" Rosa questioned.

"Not really. Please may I order a vodka and orange, a large one?"

Maybe not a wise choice but a necessary one. Rosa is looking at me without commenting, probably thinking she's seen it all before countless times.

"Please take a seat in the shade outside I will bring it to you myself."

"Thank you, Rosa."

It's a beautiful terrace, shady and surprisingly colourful with roses and other plants placed around in large, patterned plant pots. The tiled terrace is gorgeous and making me think of what changes I can make at Crumbs in the future.

"Your vodka and orange señora. Are you alright now?"

"I'm sorry Rosa it's been a very upsetting day for me." Looking into her sympathetic eyes all I can hear is Rose saying "show her the photos". She can't be here as nothing else other than that has been said but it's jolted my tired mind. Slimeball's reaction when I mentioned the Hotel Emperador of course!

"Rosa, do you have a moment to look at a photo please?"

Rosa sat at the side of me. "Sí, I have finished work."

Quickly getting Slimeball's photo larger on my screen I passed my phone to her.

"Do you recognise this man please? He has called himself several names."

"Yes, I do, he worked here for a little while. It must have been two years ago, or three, José Sanchez, yes that was his name. Why?"

I told her the short version from Wetherby and what I have learnt today. Her face has not altered, I don't know how friendly she had been with Slimeball or if they had also been an item.

"Are you going to tell the police?" Rosa asked.

"I have to, when I get back home."

"Good! He had to leave because of trouble with some older lady guests. We had complaints from the families of two ladies, wealthy ladies who lost their hearts to him and probably a lot of money as well. He ran away before they called the police. The manager can tell you more if you ask him."

"I will let the police talk to him. Thank you, Rosa you have been very kind."

"Just try to enjoy your last day tomorrow in Madrid. here is nothing more you can do for now."

"I will."

After the large vodka and orange my strength and determination to deal with this situation and also enjoy some more sightseeing tomorrow has returned. Museums, lunch and strolling down streets looking at the amazing architecture will be just what I need. It's so hot my clothes are sticking to me, the alcohol rushing through my veins won't be helping either. A cool shower, clean clothes and a stroll before something typically Spanish and delicious to eat should get me through the evening. Carol has paid for my evening meals in the hotel, and I am grateful for that. There's an aching sadness about eating alone in such a beautiful romantic city but quite acceptable in the hotel restaurant.

Showered and ready I can't make my mind up about ringing Cameron so I'm taking the coward's way out and ringing Sally first. Sally is swearing away at the other end of the phone, which is something I have never heard her do, it's funny hearing her.

"Good Lord Kate I'm sorry but this is mind-blowing news. How are you going to handle it? Don't do anything until we have both given it some thought, agreed?"

"Agreed Sally."

"Have your meal and a walk or whatever and call me again if you have decided on the course of action. There's nothing on the telly here so you're not interrupting me, okay?"

"Thanks Sally, talk soon."

I miss my solid, sensible friend and it may not be what other trippers are doing but I will get some good food and think as I eat just as she said.

Each course is a wonderful exploration of fine Spanish cuisine helped by my good waiter's advice on the different dishes. My body and brain have been fuelled well. Coffee is being brought to me on the terrace so perhaps it's still early enough to ring Sally whilst I wait, oh she's engaged. Two minutes later after trying again she's answered her phone.

"Kate I was trying to ring you, don't say anything to Pippa on Monday. If you do, she will call him, and he could do a bunk."

"That's exactly what I was going to tell you Sally. I've been making lists and there are a few people I want to talk to you when I get back on Monday. I will have to contact Cameron but that can wait too. Is he any closer with the murder at Miro, do they know who she was? He mentioned a German they are looking for, a big drug dealer."

"I'm not sure I only saw him briefly today; he's looking very tired. There's not been anything on the local news either," Sally said yawning.

"You get some sleep, everything OK at Crumbs and Flossie's okay?" I don't really need to ask when I'm so sure of the answer.

"Ticking over nicely with the girls and Mr Potter."

"Perfect, thank you. Take care."

"You too Kate."


One of the things I love about being in a different country is the smells. Shops, supermarkets, bakeries, cafés they all have a certain smell only an outsider can detect as being so "continental". My day has been packed with cultural sightseeing and I haven't been able to see half of what I wanted to. I'd love to walk through the Retiro park with someone special looking at the glasshouse, gardens and lake, perhaps I will again soon. The temperature feels too high to be out any longer so this would be a good time to head back to the hotel, have a long cool drink, no alcohol this time, and try to get hold of Cameron.

"Wake up Kitty my dear unless you want to have one leg like a lobster and the other one white."

"Good heavens Rose I swear I will have a heart attack and join you soon." My heart is racing.

"Ssssh and wipe all that dribble from the corner of your mouth, it's very unladylike," Rose tutted.

"Dribble? Oh my, did anyone see me with my mouth wide open?"

"Only half the hotel my dear. I suggest you whisper before they really start to get concerned."

"Right, yes, well I'm tired after today. I was enjoying my drink in the shade before ringing Cameron, but I must have fallen asleep."

"Over an hour ago my dear and if you are going to call him, think first how you can still help Pippa, would it not be better to wait until you have got back to Crumbs? After all there's not much he can do on a Sunday night. Kate, I have warned you, this could be bigger than you realise please slow down. Before I get all the arguing from you, go over your lists, you will get inspiration and then do get a shower, you are beginning to smell like wilting flowers my dear."

Those were Rose's parting words. Wilting flowers indeed, a quick look around and a sniff of my armpits suggests another victory for Rose!

# Chapter Fifteen

A weekend is not long enough for a trip abroad, but much as I love what I have experienced, I'm glad to be on the train just about to be pulling into Leeds City station.

Rain is bouncing off the pavements, running down the outer edges of the roads towards City Square searching for any unblocked drain to escape down. Thankfully the Queens Hotel is next door to the train station. No red carpet out on the front steps today, still I never informed them of my arrival.

Pippa is already seated with her shopping bags from Harvey Nichols and several other top designer shops lined up at the side of her plush chair.

"You have been busy Pippa," trying my broadest smile to cover up the panic rising in my throat up to my face.

Pippa jumped up and flung her arms around me, covering me in Coco Chanel perfume. Seems to be a certain aged lady wears it and all wear it well. Please help me to get her home without blurting it all out, I need a little more time first.

My silent prayer must have worked. Either that,

or my ranting like someone who has been on a desert island for the last 10 years and just found their voice and someone to talk to other than a turtle has kept Pippa quiet. I did of course let her talk about her plans, it would have been rude not to, but I nodded or cooed in the right places without commenting.

Walking into the underground car park of the Queens Hotel I'm suddenly thrown off balance by the fact we are going home in Slimeball's car and not Pippa's.

"Just throw your bag on the back seat Kate, my "Rangie" is in for service so it's quite handy having Antonio's to fall back on."

"When is he back from the South?" I have to know how much time I have left, the flaming liar.

"He's trying for Wednesday night. It depends if there are any pressing meetings to follow up on."

Pressing! The only pressing he will be doing is the sheets! Sorry Gran, but it's true.

Inside his car smells like the perfumery department in one of the large stores at Christmas. Pippa's and Slimeball's aromas all mixed up and yet quite distinguishable, Coco and Brummel, to be expected as he is Spanish. Will she notice if I open my window at all?

I'm trying to be noncommittal as Pippa talks non-stop about the wedding arrangements, thank goodness we are passing through Collingham, not far now to Wetherby. We are home!

"Are you coming in Pippa?"

"Do you mind if I dash off Kate? I've been out all day and I must check on Davenport Manor. Have a good rest tonight and we'll talk tomorrow, bye sweetie," Pippa said blowing a kiss.

"Thank you for everything, bye."

Flossie is so excited at seeing me, there's no love like a pet's love. Sally and the girls as cheerful as always have rushed to help me with my bag and wet coat.

"Do you want a drink bringing upstairs or are you going to have a rest?" Sally asked hugging me.

"I'll just dump my bag and freshen up, there's only 30 minutes until closing and I'd like to help you."

I really don't think I could rest even if someone tucked me up and sang me a lullaby. My head is swimming with questions and a horrible nagging fear of the next few days.

No more customers have braved the downpour of rain. I've closed Crumbs so the girls can go home early, Sally wants to stay in talk. With Flossie at my feet, hot drinks and biscuits in front of us, I really don't know where to begin.

Listening intently to the whole sordid story, Sally has remained silent throughout. She would make a good detective or surveillance person.

"Have you got your phone downstairs Kate; I'd better see the photos? On second thoughts it may be advisable to send them to me as well, we should have a backup of them just in case."

She's right. The more I've thought about it all

the darker and deeper it gets.

"Good Lord Almighty! The swine, how many others has he put through this? You don't have much time Kate so tomorrow you will have to see Pippa. Tomorrow is Tuesday, he could be back by Wednesday at the latest."

"I know, it's making me feel sick thinking about him coming back. Do you think Cameron should be told tonight or will tomorrow do?"

"Do you feel up to telling him right now? I'm not sure if he is around here or working in Leeds on your friends' case, we haven't seen or heard from him for a few days."

"I'll text him later then he can answer in his own time. Sally, you get home and thank you my friend for everything. See you tomorrow, not too early I can manage first thing on my own." I'm squeezing her tightly, I'm so grateful to be with them all again.

Half an hour later the floor has been mopped, all the crockery and cutlery emptied from the dishwasher and in their right order on the shelves and drawers. There has been so little to do I'm mentally adding extra money to their pay packets. Good reliable staff are hard to find, I am so lucky.

"Flossie come on girl let's go upstairs for a little rest, I'll put the television on for you."

Flossie came bounding down the garden path having been behind the shed for her tiddle.

"Woof."

"OK Flossie, will lovely Jessica Fletcher and

Murder, She Wrote suit you?"

"Woof."

"I thought so."

Flossie has settled herself on her favourite large cushion in front of my TV. I have strict rules about beds, it's for me only, for now anyway. My small black leather holdall is on the floor where I dumped it waiting for me to unpack but all I need for now are my wash bag and makeup bag, the rest can wait. My whole body feels restless and unlike Flossie I can't settle. What I need is a good soak in my own bath, bubbles up to my neck, some thinking and relaxing time.

Stripping off my travelling clothes I suddenly feel so much easier. Stepping over Flossie to get my holdall for my wash bag, she has quickly put one paw over her eyes.

"Very funny my girl! It's nothing you haven't seen before!" I'm laughing. Flossie always manages to make me laugh when I'm feeling low. "You concentrate on solving the mystery with Jessica Fletcher then you can help me solve this one here in Wetherby."

"Woof."

Reaching for my luggage my hand has suddenly frozen in mid-air just above the two leather handles on my holdall. In fact, my whole body feels frozen with massive hair lifting goosebumps from my head to my toes. I can't touch it, I must not touch anything, instinct tells me not to. The two long leather handles are usually held together in the middle by a strip of leather which is stitched to one of the handles. Velcro is on the edges of the piece of leather. I always wrap the strip of leather with Velcro fastening around the middle of the two handles to keep them together when I carry the bag, but this time I didn't, or it had come undone. Stuck to the Velcro are two long blue strands of silky material, identical to the fringe on the poor murder victim's scarf left in Miro!

Bile has rushed upwards into my throat making me leap over Flossie and dive into the bathroom, head down the loo just in the nick of time. Beads of sweat have broken out on my forehead and within seconds have gone cold making me shiver and my teeth chatter. Anyone would think I have flu; no this is far worse.

What the hell am I going to do? Keep calm, breathe, that's it breathe, get my bare backside off this cold floor for a start and some warm clothes on. Flossie has brought my phone in her mouth and is looking at me with her head on an angle.

"Thank you, Flossie, I'm alright girl or I think I will be. I'll ring Cameron but Pippa, I have to speak to Pippa, oh and Sally. Sorry I'm gabbling Flossie."

"Woof."

Cameron's phone went to his voicemail, so I left what I hope is a coherent message. Sally next only she's halfway round Morrisons supermarket with all her family helping her. Sally will call when she returns home.

I don't want to waste the bath full of bubbles.

With my phone on a stool at the side of the bath I'm going to wash the travel grime away quickly and get dressed to be ready, for what I'm not sure yet, all I know is nothing can be tackled fully naked.

Still no answer from Cameron and I'm not sure if I should ring the Wetherby police station, I only want to talk to Cameron. The doorbell is ringing, not many people ring my back doorbell.

"Come on Flossie, time to look fierce girl."

Flossie is down the steps and barking like a mad dog at the back door.

"Who is it?" I'm trying to sound in control but it's hard to be when in reality I feel like a blob of jelly on a plate.

"Kate it's me, Pippa."

That door has never been yanked open so fast. I can sense the distress in her voice without even seeing her face. Goodness me Pippa looks a total wreck! Black streaks of mascara are running down her perfect foundation and her nose is threatening to chase it.

"Come in, whatever is the matter? Here let me take your wet coat, I'll get us some hot drinks."

"I'm sorry to come to you like this but I didn't know what else to do. There's only you I can talk to." Pippa sobbed in my arms, heart breaking, gulping sobs shaking her slim body. My God, she must have found something out about him to affect her this badly, but how much?

"Woof, woof." Flossie has brought the tissue box

and dropped it at Pippa's feet.

"Thank you, Flossie," she said crying and tearing out tissues.

"Come on sit down Pippa with Flossie whilst I bring the coffee, strong?"

"Yes please," she said managing to smile between blowing her nose. By the time the cafetière and the slices of cherry and almond cake are across the table, Pippa has composed herself enough to eat and drink the strong coffee. I'm waiting for her to talk first.

"I saw him," is all she said.

I'm too afraid to ask, coward that I am. If I ask, then all this horrible sordid nightmare will unravel. It has to, and it will, but I don't want to be the one to break this lovely lady's heart. Oh, get a grip, I'm not the one breaking people's hearts, Slimeball is!

Pippa dived forward and grabbed my hand with both of hers. "I'm not going mad Kate, but I saw him tonight sitting there in his favourite chair in the office, large as life, but he can't be can he? Alive I mean, because I know he's dead."

Oh Lord, this is worse than I thought, she's found out and killed him, not that he doesn't deserve it. When and how? Pippa hasn't had much time since she dropped me off, keep calm, time to listen and not react. Inwardly I'm so tense even my muscles are screaming.

Pippa looked up with more tears in her eyes, foundation practically non-existent. "Humphrey, my darling Humph, the one and only love of my life," looking at my puzzled expression. "Humphrey Davenport my last husband, Davenport Manor Hotel."

At last, the penny dropped with me and I'm ashamed to say swathed me in relief all over my tense body.

"I'm sorry Pippa I was slightly confused as I never knew your husband."

"No, of course you didn't. Dear Humphrey, he was just wonderful, kind, loving but as they say the good always die young. It was his heart for many years, good years." The tears fell again.

"Did he speak to you?"

"He did, I don't know what to do because of what he said."

I let her compose herself. As she spoke, I knew it had been a good marriage full of love and mutual respect. Humphrey did not want her to part with any money for Slimeballs' restaurant. Well done, Humphrey!

"Did he say anything else to do with Antonio?" I asked with all my fingers crossed. I honestly feel this needs to be looked into more and only the police will know how much he is involved in. We can't scare Pippa or warn him off.

"No, but Humphrey never spoke badly of anyone, he was a very fair person. I just don't feel I should do anything straight away. Antonio is rushing me too much and Humphrey has made me realise that now."

"Look Pippa you have possibly two more days before he gets back, wait, don't say anything if he rings you. Have you had any more texts whilst I was away?"

"Several and all of them are warnings, not vicious. Now I'm wondering who it is and what else they know that I don't," Pippa said anxiously.

"I'm speaking to Cameron so I will mention it, that's if you don't mind."

"Please do and I will try to stay busy and keep a little out of reach tonight and tomorrow, except to you two. Thank you for listening and not thinking me to be a mad woman seeing ghosts."

"My childhood was full of spiritual stuff because of my Gran and Rose being big believers in the afterlife. I've had my fair share of the unexplained so please don't worry, talk to me anytime you want if you get any further sightings and messages."

Pippa hugged me and held me tightly for a while before leaving. She is still a mixture of sad, scared and yet I feel she is stronger in a way, I hope she continues in that way as tomorrow or the next day she has a heck of a lot more to face up to.

"ROSE!! If you are around, please come!" I'm shouting, I don't know why, frustration probably.

"Don't shout my dear, I was here all the time, quietly watching and listening."

"I knew you were behind the Humphrey visitation, well this time I will let you off. Thank you, Pippa needs his advice. How did you find him with all the others up there?" I'm pointing up to heaven.

"Well, that is easy my dear Kitty, Humphrey is in my poker club and also an active member of our Anti Ghostbusters club, nice chap. We often meet up in Monaco at the casino for a bit of fun."

I've opened my mouth to comment but I reckon it's pointless. "Well thank you both and please continue to protect and advise in any way you can."

"Yes, and as always my dear take care, wait for Cameron to do the investigating. It's far too dangerous. Most fly, toodle pip."

Silence has descended around us but this time I wish she had stayed longer to listen to me.

# Chapter Sixteen

With still no call back from Cameron I'm getting edgy, I can't just sit here, there are two people I need to speak to. Sally rang and is up to date with this evening so hopefully she can keep trying Cameron for me.

Susan Walsh's Westminster doorbell chimes, figures as she is a Southerner born and bred. This is awful I feel like a drowned rat and Flossie looks like one. The pair of us are dripping all over her front doorstep. The sound of several locks being undone before her heavy-duty door opens and Susan is standing in a pair of penguin slippers looking at us in surprise. That's a lot of security but perhaps Susan has the right idea, and I should think along the same lines.

"Ooh Kate and poor little Flossie, come in, come in. Give me your coat Kate, it can dry out in the kitchen. Tea or coffee or perhaps a little brandy or whisky?" Susan winked.

"Tea will be fine, thank you. I'm sorry to come on such a terrible evening but what I need to ask can't wait until tomorrow."

"Come through with Flossie. Clive is in the lounge, but you know him and it's really no trouble at all."

"Do I? I don't think I've met Clive." The words are still on my lips as Susan shows me into a very pretty lounge and Clive is standing to greet me. All my birthdays have come together, it's Mr Greaves, the two people I need to speak to under one roof.

My main aim is to try and find out why Susan reacted the way she did in Crumbs and if Clive, Mr Greaves, will open up to me about the threat I witnessed. My gut instincts tell me there is more to it all and that the jigsaw puzzle will have a few more pieces to connect with what they say.

Flossie has curled up at my feet with her front paws over her eyes. To anyone who doesn't know her well she appears to have settled down for a dog nap, no, her right ear is up, taking in every word.

I have had to explain a few things to Susan and Mr Greaves without revealing too much, just enough to help them to open up. Susan's story is heart wrenching and Mr Greaves, although reluctant at first to say much, warmed as I explained how I recognised his knee problem. Once he started to disclose more his relief became evident, like confessing to a priest. The difference being he does understand I have to repeat it all to Cameron.

Walking back to Crumbs in the torrential rain I feel quite sad that this lovely market town is just as corrupt and pitted with evil as Leeds or any other large city. How sad that evil can penetrate all corners of our island.

Parked outside the garden gate to Crumbs is a dark car I'm not familiar with. The hairs on the back of my neck have sprung up. I've got to stop panicking but until the police have been told everything I know and some kind of investigation into Slimeball is started, I have to be cautious. Flossie is ahead of me, alert as always, now her tail is wagging! Okay let's have a look at who is in the driver's seat, steaming up a small section of his window.

Now I can't stop laughing! Cameron's nose is squashed against the window, his mouth open, snoring away. Poor thing, he's absolutely worn out. Sally said as much and looking through the rain he certainly looks deep in sleep.

"Woof," Flossie is trying to say "hello".

Cameron has jerked upright in his seat and is quickly wiping some drool from the side of his mouth and chin, I've been there many times myself.

"Hello, sorry to wake you up, well Flossie did not me."

"That's fine, I'll forgive you as long as you feed me some of your wonderful cake and plenty of coffee to keep me going."

"It's a deal."

If it were not for the serious reason Cameron is visiting, I could get used to sitting opposite him whilst he enjoys my baking. Outside the rain is still pelting down. According to the weather reports, if this continues, we will get flooding around the

Wetherby and York areas. The rivers have caused so much damage over the last few years for both homeowners and farmers.

Cameron is chasing the last few crumbs of his jam and coconut cake with his cake fork. He has placed it on his plate with a cheeky contented smile.

"Thank you, that was delicious, you know the way to my heart," he said cheerfully.

Wow! If only.

"Now to the serious stuff. Sally has told me; can you go into more detail Kate please? Take it step by step whilst I write it all down and the photos you took as well, please."

"Still no further with any identification in Leeds of the poor soul murdered at Miro?"

"Not quite."

Not quite, that's not an answer but then he doesn't have to reveal anything to me, a civilian. It's a good job I made my lists and notes to jog my memory as I'm telling him.

Cameron only interrupted a few times to ask more about Slimeball's time in Aranjuez and the hotel in Madrid, the rest of the time he filled his pages with notes.

"I've been thinking Cameron, why would the lady the waiter thought was Antonio's wife be called a foreigner by Antonio?"

"What do you mean?"

"Well, if she was a Spaniard, he would not refer to her as a foreigner as she was from the same country as him."

"I see what you mean now, in fact that's a good point, thank you."

After a bit more scribbling Cameron closed his notebook and looked at me with a serious expression clouding his beautiful dark eyes and handsome face.

"What's wrong?"

"Kate, you have done a great job getting all this information, it will help a lot. Poor Pippa will have to be told and she will need a friend to talk to after but I'm afraid of you putting yourself in any danger if we don't pick him up straight away."

"Cameron, I haven't finished yet."

"No?" he asked with his eyebrows up.

"I've just seen Susan Walsh and Mr Greaves; you will have to interview them both as they are both connected with all this. I suspected they were, and I was right. Susan recognised Pippa's engagement ring when they came in here to show me it. She also recognised Antonio as the Spaniard who got engaged to her widowed friend in Bournemouth several years ago."

"With the ruby ring?" Cameron cut in.

"The one and same. Her friend gave him a substantial amount of money left to her by her husband as an investment. She never saw him or her money again, or the ring. Apparently, Susan's friend was so distraught she drove her car over the cliff edge, or did she? Goodness knows how many women have worn that ring over the years. Poor

Mr Greaves is another matter altogether, that's pure blackmail."

"Goodness Kate what else are you involved in?"

I'm looking into his eyes and trying to sound sensible when deep inside I'm quaking. Talking it over with a policeman makes it all the more real and scary.

"Mr Greaves likes fashion, ladies fashion."

"Yes, and?"

"Mr Greaves likes to buy all the fashionable clothes and wear them."

"Oh, I see."

"All the busybodies here thought he had different women coming out of his house, different coloured hair, smartly dressed but all with the same knee problem as Mr Greaves."

"So how did Mr alias Antonio Lopez know?"

"He saw him in a hotel in Leeds and realised he could blackmail him. It's obvious that Mr Greaves and Susan are good friends who support and protect each other. Judging by the impact Antonio has had on their lives I think you will get her to reveal she is the one trying to warn Pippa by text."

"I understand, the texts I was shown on Pippa's phone were never threatening, always warnings," he nodded as he recalled the nature of the texts. "I can see them both tonight and wait until I've been back to the station to interview Pippa. He's coming back on Wednesday you said?"

"So we believe, and hope. We need more time to be able to tell all this to Pippa. She's in a bad enough state about the money, I dare not tell her anything without telling you what I have found out first."

"You did right Kate, so is that absolutely everything?"

"No."

"Oh, why am I not surprised at that answer?" he said with a glint in his eyes.

"It's just something I have to show you which could tie in with the murder at Miro, well maybe."

"Kate, what have you done now?"

"Nothing, honestly, all I did was throw my holdall onto the back seat of the car when Pippa picked me up from the train station today."

"Now you have totally lost me."

"Pippa had borrowed the car belonging to Antonio or whoever he really is because he's away and Pippa's is in the garage. When I went to get my wash bag out tonight, I noticed something important. Let me get it and you will see; I haven't touched it."

"Then it will be better if I come upstairs with you."

My heart has turned over! Oh, come on Kate, he saw you in all your worst only the other week, in your bedroom. Pull yourself together girl.

"Woof."

"OK Flossie." Strewth even my dog can read minds, this is getting too crazy. All I need now is Rose twittering in my ear, talk about being chaperoned.

I showed him the blue silky strands stuck to

my Velcro strap. He looked slightly puzzled, in a handsome way.

"Do you remember the blue pashmina I found behind the sofa in Miro?" Cameron nodded. "There were about three strands of the fringe missing at one end of the pashmina. I'm almost sure they are the same material as the fringe."

After a few moments of awkward silence Cameron reached into his jacket pocket for some gloves and a bag then carefully removed and sealed the strands inside the bag.

"Kate, I truly do not know how you do it. If you are right, and it certainly looks like it then this is a major lead," he said, his dark brown eyes lingering on mine.

In that split second, I was sure he was going to move forward and hold me, even kiss me, but he suddenly stepped backwards.

"I have to get this to Forensics in Leeds before it's too late," he said heading from the staircase to Crumbs' kitchen.

By the time I had joined him downstairs he had phoned in and was heading for the back door, bag in hand and a slight flush on his face.

"Kate, I'm worried this is a major breakthrough thanks to you, but it also creates major concerns for your safety. Please don't go out alone or let anyone in tonight. If anything happened to you I..." he didn't finish his sentence.

"I'm not alone I have Flossie," I tried to say confidently.

"Woof."

As soon as Cameron had driven away it dawned on me, something the waiter in Aranjuez has said could tie in with what my dear friend Al at Miro had noticed. Al, a lover of women, notices shoes and feet, amongst other things but then that's just Al. The gap between the big toe and the first toe on her right foot, some might say that is not "normal". It strikes me that Slimeball looks for perfection so why marry someone who wasn't perfect? Maybe he didn't have a choice as in a family member holding a shotgun to his head if he didn't. I can't expect to speak to Cameron, but I can text him all the information just in case.

"Flossie, look at this weather, the roses in the garden will be ruined if this continues. Can you go for a tiddle behind the shed and we can stay warm and dry upstairs tonight?"

"Woof."


"Good morning, Sally, you're bright and early on such a miserable day. Fancy some toast? I was just about to make myself a few slices."

"Go on then you've twisted my arm, one white please. How can I ever keep my weight down working here, it's impossible."

"Come off it Sally, Chris loves your cuddly figure." I can't help but smile at my redhead cuddly friend.

"Talking of love, did Cameron come last night?

Come on dish up the gossip with my tea and toast."

I filled Sally in with last night's events whilst she chewed with wide eyes.

"It's Pippa I'm worried about. Slimeball could have got rid of at least two ladies and he somehow managed to get the ring back and reinvent himself elsewhere. He could be a serial killer, Sally."

"Good Lord, I see what you mean. He's supposed to be coming back tomorrow, let's hope they get him at the airport as soon as he lands. Right lady, there's not much else you can do now just leave it to the police. What would you like me to do here as I'm early and with all this heavy rain we will be quiet first thing?"

"Could you whip me some cream please Sally? Use three tubs so we have enough for the scones and cakes. I will get started on slicing the Madeira, cranberry and orange and the coconut loaf cakes then do the gateaux."

Only four customers in half an hour, this rain is bad for business. Oh, here come Miss Hall and Miss Winters.

"Nice to see you ladies, don't let the weather ruin your get togethers. Let me take your coats and umbrellas."

"Thank you, Kate," they said in unison.

Orders taken; Sally has busied herself getting the teapots filled whilst I toast the currant teacakes. Sally served and I carried on with decorating the cakes, one Black Forest gateau and one peach and raspberry gateau. Plenty of cream and fruit.

"Whew! You went to town on the kirsch in the Black Forest gateau this time! It's beautiful and strong with a generous amount of black cherries. If any is left, I'll take home a couple of portions for Chris, he loves it."

"No problem."

Suddenly Sally is by my side and pulling on her ear lobe flashing her eyes towards the ladies' table, our code for us to listen.

"I've not seen that flashy chap of Pippa Davenport's for a while Jean, have you? Maybe he's done a runner with all her money, he looks shifty enough."

"They say he's been away on business leaving her to do all the wedding arrangements, funny business more like. Due back tomorrow by all accounts only I could have sworn I saw him get out of a white car this morning. He didn't have a crutch so I must be mistaken," Miss Hall answered in between bites of teacake.

"More tea, Jean?"

"Yes, please Peggy."

My blood ran cold when I heard her. "Sally I must ring Pippa. Cameron could still be with her that way they will both be warned.

Pippa's phone went straight to her voicemail, so I've asked her to call me back.

"If it is him back early it has to mean he knows the police are after him. This is awful Sally I feel so helpless."

"Kate calm down please. First of all, you don't know it is him, she could be mistaken and then Pippa should know about him from Cameron by now so she will call the police if he turns up. Hotels have plenty of people around, she's hardly on her own in the building."

"I'm sorry Sally, I'll keep trying Cameron's phone too."

"Talk of the devil and he appears," Sally said cheerfully.

"Wow are you psychic?" I asked spinning around to find Sally being kissed by Cameron, me next please, oh well one day soon.

"I just popped in for a quick drink after seeing Pippa. In answer to your next question, because I'm psychic, she is shocked of course but anybody would be after what I had to tell her. A part of her was beginning to have doubts, question a few things she had found out herself. She's going to play along with him when he turns up and let us know when he's there. Until I get the results on the silk strands, we can only bring him in for the false identities and money from the ladies and blackmail. We've sent out information across the country, we could be adding more charges to his list. I have a feeling he'll sing like a canary when we get him to the station."

Cameron's phone rang and he walked away to take the call.

My hands feel like I've been in a sauna, all sweaty. It's not good news I can tell by his worried expression. He's calling to Sally and I to go back into the kitchen with him.

"They are a match."

"I knew it!" Don't let me weaken, please keep me standing upright. Filling a glass with cold water and taking several gulps I'm desperately hanging onto the kitchen sink with the constant rain pouring onto the window, flowing like tears down the glass. My brain is saying "here you go again, you asked for it with your snooping, stop weakening, stay strong." Turning back to face him I'm aware of his strained face, telling me there's more to come.

"We traced him to Nice then on to Monaco. The woman he went with is still there, they're interviewing her now. Apparently, he left in a hurry, urgent business back home but as yet there's been no flight taken in his names that we know of."

"Do you know anything more about the murder at Miro, who she is, or was?" That sounded so awful, "was" that is all she has become, the once beautiful lady with the pashmina.

"Your information was correct. I've been told she was his wife for seven years, no children which is a blessing. She was a Colombian living in Barcelona and working in an art gallery there. Something in her life must have set her on a trail to find him, and it cost her a lot more than she expected."

Sally topped up his coffee and he sipped it

thoughtfully.

My mind is whirring at one hundred miles an hour. Images flashing in front of my eyes.

"Cameron, I keep seeing the ring, it all evolves around the ring. Maybe it was his wife's, an heirloom and he took it with him when he left her. I can't see him giving it to his wife as an engagement ring, does Spain have that custom? He was mainly working as a waiter and that ruby ring smacks of quality, and money. Good Lord! Pippa has the ring. Cameron he could be here in Wetherby already. We just overheard Miss Hall say she thought she'd seen him get out of a white car."

Cameron put down his cup, grabbing my shoulders and looking deep into my eyes.

"Kate, stay safe, please. I have to go; Sally talk some sense into her will you please?"

"I'll try but it could be like winning the lottery, who knows if it will work."

Cameron didn't hear Sally as he has dashed out of the kitchen door before the words have evaporated.

Customers came in soggy and went back out dry, happier for having had a drink, a slice of cake and a chat to break the monotony of the dreary day. It is sometime before 4:00 PM and the door swung open with force. Pippa is standing shaking her umbrella furiously before entering. Dressed in a deep green full length waterproof coat with a hood, she looks as chic as ever - except for her ashen face. I'm beckoning to her to come straight through to the back of the kitchen away from the prying eyes and straining ears of any customers. Sally has started the coffee machine and got the tray ready signalling to me to go upstairs with her and she will bring it up. I'm smiling my thank you at Sally.

"Come on Pippa, we'll go upstairs."

Pippa silently obliged.

"How are you?" as soon as the words were out, I could have kicked myself, of course she feels devastated, who wouldn't?

"Numb. Finding out about the money was bad enough, but I would still have given him a chance. After Cameron had gone this morning, my mind felt it would explode then Cameron rang me about the two ladies, my poor Humphrey would be so ashamed of me," Pippa is gulping with tears flowing fast down her cheeks.

"No, he wouldn't, he wanted you to be happy again. This is just an evil person taking advantage of your good heart."

Pippa thrust her hands deep into a pocket inside her coat and pulled out a ring box.

"Here Kate please can you give it to Cameron. I can't face having it at the Manor and I don't want to walk into Wetherby police station. All these people knowing what an old fool I have been," she sobbed again.

Sally came up with the coffee and cake on a tray. She's putting it on my bedside table and hugging Pippa before dashing back downstairs

"If you're sure about me taking it, I will."

As soon as Pippa put the ring box in my hand all the hairs on the back of my neck of spring upon end. Gran would have been able to sense so much just by holding it.

Pippa wanted to know how I have found so much out about Slimeball in Spain and of course what I had witnessed in the airport. I've tried to skirt around that a little, because she's hurting too much, thank goodness she didn't ask any more about the other woman.

There's only so much talking someone with a broken heart can do, take it from one who has been there big time. I tried to explain this to Sally. Your life's force seems to have been sucked out of your body and an amount of personal space is often just what is needed to get your head straight.

My new dilemma is where can I stash the ring? We do have a small safe of sorts for Crumbs' daily takings. Thinking as a thief or should I say Slimeball that would be the most obvious place to look, so where? Glancing around the kitchen my eyes are resting on a teapot. Not the ones we use daily, this is a special one of three on another shelf above the others. Gran's Susie Cooper teapot with a pink crocus design, her pride and joy from her young days. Perfect!

"Where are you putting it, no, surely not in there?" Sally is asking with a slight giggle. "Won't your Gran object to the intrusion?"

"No, she'll just have to move over a tiny bit, and

Rose as well."

"I didn't realise Rose was watching me from up there all this time."

"Rose watches from all over this place she doesn't miss a trick, honestly." One day I will tell Sally, just not at the moment. The two small boxes containing some of their ashes have sat side by side in the teapot undisturbed until now. I'm sure it will be safe there; they were both forces to be reckoned with in life so why not now?

# Chapter Seventeen

Grabbing my phone, I can see it's Pippa calling.

"He's been here Kate, I know it, I smelled his aftershave in my bedroom when I got home from Crumbs," Pippa is gabbling tearfully.

"Have you rung the police?"

"Yes, they have told me to stay behind reception where there are so many guests sitting around drinking, to be seen by others is safer."

"I think that is wise, please stay there I'm sure he can't do anything in front of the others. Let me know what the police say. I can come over later if you want or stay overnight if it helps."

"Oh, thank you Kate, I will let you know. Please take care yourself."

Mopping floors always helps my grey cells kick in and at the moment they have accelerated into full speed.

"Slow down my dear Kitty or you are in danger of washing the pattern off the floor," Rose piped up from high.

"Rose there never was a pattern on the floor," I'm searching hard above me to the right.

"Not that side Kitty, I've moved behind you on the far table. You really must learn how to zoom into my voice better than you do."

"Thank you for the redirection, to what do I owe this visitation?" I'm tired, worried and certainly not in the mood for my ghostly godmother.

"You tickled my toes Kitty," Rose said giggling.

"*Pardon*? How an earth could *I* have tickled your toes? Oh, I get it, you are trying to tell me I have your feet in that box." Not a nice thought but then nothing has ever entered my head before regarding the boxes and which body parts I am keeping.

"Not feet my dear, toes, my right big, second and little toes to be precise."

Rose always was a precise person, no edging around things just straight and to the point.

"Alright, so sorry if I disturbed your time but I thought it is the safest place for now to put that dreadful ring."

"No, my dear I would not class it as dreadful. It's not to your taste or indeed mine either but it is extremely valuable and quite safe between your Gran and me. You my dear are not safe if he finds out how you discovered who murdered his wife."

"Rose I will be careful, promise. When I've done all the cleaning and preparations for tomorrow, Flossie and I will walk to Davenport Manor Hotel and stay overnight if Pippa needs us to. Nothing can happen there. She has called the police again and if you think about it, I will be far safer there amongst other people. The police are bound to pick him up tomorrow if he returns."

"Well get there quickly before it starts getting dark and stay with Pippa or in your locked bedroom. You will be the death of me Kitty."

"Again?"

All I can hear is Rose tutting. I'll blow her a kiss to soften her as I always did when she was here.

"Watch her every move Flossie, I'll not be far away, bye bye my dear."

"Woof," barked Flossie.

"Bye Rose, thank you."

Covered up in my waterproof jacket, waterproof over trousers and with a few overnight things in a small, zipped bag plus some extra treats for Flossie, we are ready to go out into the rain. I may not look as stylish as Pippa but at least I'm fairly protected. Flossie on the other hand is getting drenched again. If I had brought her doggy shampoo with me, I could have given her a good shampoo on route. It's her own fault she hates the all in one suit I bought her, can't say I blame her though, it is very poncified.

This is lighter rain than before but it's still coming down fast leaving more puddles than path to walk along. The river to the left of me is roaring past with broken branches from trees charging like canoes through rapids. Good job I don't have any mascara on because my face is wet through.

"Careful Flossie, don't go off too far, keep near me girl."

"Woof."

We have reached the car park alongside the river

which even after 6:00 PM on a summer's evening is normally full of cars. People would be walking by the river feeding the ducks or picnicking by the water. Today there are only three empty cars parked. I've always found it strange how drivers, when given an almost empty car park, will often "cuddle" up next to another car, safety in numbers perhaps. Sure enough that's the case tonight, red, white and a blue like a flag.

The water is particularly fast here as there is a weir a bit further along. Another day and night of this rain and the river will break its banks and flood the car park, it's happened many times before. Somewhere ahead of us further along the path I can hear voices. I can't quite make out whether they are just talking loudly because of the roar from the water or they're arguing. There is another sound over the top of the voices, it's Flossie growling and barking fiercely. In these situations, it must be similar to a mother protecting her child, Flossie is my child, for now, and I know I have to get to her quickly.

I'm trying my best to run through the rain and the deep puddles with my bag hampered by my stupid hood which keeps falling over my eyes. There's a man, a runner all in black charging towards me, wet through, his black hat pulled far down onto his face. Flossie is at his heels snapping away, her teeth and gums showing as she snarls.

"Flossie come here girl, now!"

As the man in black runs alongside me he has

suddenly struck out his arm with such a powerful force hitting me full on the right side of my jaw and eye, knocking me sideways. The trees are swirling around me. I'm falling, good Lord I'm going down the slippery, muddy banking to the river.

"Help! Help! Please help me!"

In the split seconds of sliding all I can do to desperately stop myself is to dig my fingers into the muddy banking. Roots! There are roots! It's working, there's one sticking out which I've managed to grasp in my right hand, please, please let that be another one, thank you! The roots I'm hanging onto are not very thick and my feet are both in the fast-flowing river making it difficult to stay straight and get a foothold on the banking. The water wants to take me with it.

Above me somewhere to the right there is shouting again, swearing, why can't they hear me and help?

"Help! I need some help here!"

Good Lord, I can't do it I'm slipping. Each time I try to get my waterlogged foot up it's just not able to grip onto the grassy steep slope for the slippery mud. This is it; I know this is the end for me, I'll drown, I know this is it!

"Rose, Gran don't let me die this way, please! Help me, Flossie make them come please."

Flossie is running up and down barking in a high pitch, she's tried to get to me but can't, my poor little friend is going to see me drown. There's a woman's voice shouting as well. I'm losing the little strength I had, I'm sorry it's no good, I'm falling further. I really can't hang on much longer, I know I can't. Suddenly Rose's voice is calling out to me.

"You can Kitty, just a little longer, try and lift your feet out of the water, you can do it please hang on."

I'm trying to lift them one at a time to stop me being dragged along the fast-flowing water. That's one foot up onto the banking. If my strength holds out it's better than before.

"Aaaah!"

Good Lord what's that? There's suddenly an ear-piercing bloodcurdling scream to my right cutting through the roar of the river. The figure in black is hurtling through the air, arms and legs thrashing hopelessly before crashing into the swollen raging dark water. Voices above me are shouting again but this time it's to me and a lady's voice has joined in with a man's voice.

"Kate, Kate, grab this branch quickly."

Looking up through my muddy hair and streaming tears there is my lifeline, a thick branch held by Mr Greaves. I'm trying frantically with all my strength but it's not long enough to reach me. I can't grab the end; all I keep getting are leaves and sharp brittle twigs cutting into my hand.

"Try again, come on Kate try again, you have to try harder, don't give up."

Pulling with all my strength on the roots in my

left hand and pushing the toe of my right trainer into the muddy banking my body has lurched forward and upward slightly. I've got it, dear Lord thank you I've got it!

Another person has run up behind Mr Greaves. Two stronger male hands have taken over the branch.

"Get behind me Mr Greaves, grab my coat and keep pulling me back up to the path whilst I pull Kate out," Cameron is shouting to Mr Greaves.

Working like two people in a tug of war team their combined strength is bringing me out of my watery grave. They have done it; they have saved me! My head is spinning, every part of me is shaking and my legs feel like jelly. Oh no I'm going to be sick!

In times of extreme emotional stress, the weakest part of me has always been my stomach. I can't help it whether it's going to a wedding (which let's face it none so far have been a great success including my own) or sitting exams, I heave, boy do I heave. Some say it's because my star sign is Gemini, I don't know. All I do know is that this is the second time in just over a month Cameron has rescued me whilst I'm looking my worst. Unfazed by my hair and face caked in mud and quite possibly sick he has just held me tightly and wiped my mouth with Susan's hand wipes. I want to go home!

"Come on let's get you and Flossie back home. Mr Greaves and Miss Walsh, I will need to take a statement from you both later. You did witness it all and you do know who did this don't you? I'll be over to you in an hour Mr Greaves, okay?"

"Yes, we do know, we will both stay at my house until you need us," Mr Greaves said.

"Thank you, all of you," is all I could manage to shakily say.

Cameron has produced two large plastic bags from the boot of his car, one for my muddy coat and one for me to sit on. I imagine his car boot is full of all the necessary bags, boots and spades for cases. Soggy trousers and soggy knickers are not helping. Goodness me I'm actually terrified to move on the plastic bag for fear it makes another squelching noise. Flossie is curled up on the mat on the floor behind my passenger seat, one ear twitching.

"I just need to call this in Kate and get a team out along the river. He could be anywhere from the weir to Tadcaster or on to where the river Wharfe meets the river Ouse at York," Cameron said as he unlocked the screen of his mobile.

"If it is Antonio then he can't swim, Pippa told me."

That's really bothering me, but I don't want to say too much at the moment. Why would someone who can't swim jump into deep fast flowing water? They wouldn't! Cameron has just pulled up outside my back gate and is looking at me with his handsome face full of concern. Why the heck are all the tender moments because of my near-death situations? This is pure madness.

"Are you sure you don't want me to get Sally over?"

"No, thank you, I'll be fine after I've soaked for a while in the bath. I'll talk to Sally later. Are you contacting Pippa?"

"When I've taken the statements from Mr Greaves and Miss Walsh. Let's get the whole picture sorted out first."

"Before you go, how did you know to come to the river?"

"An older lady with grey curly hair came running up to me in Davenport Manor Hotel and said you were in danger of drowning in between the trees at the car park. I just ran to my car and drove fast to the river car park. Kate, you scared me, are you always going to be scaring me?" Cameron said touching my face.

"If you let me, I will."

"I will," he said smiling.


News travels fast in Wetherby, not always the correct news but when it goes around so many people it's bound to get over exaggerated. I'm saying nothing until Cameron has told me what went on by the water. The ruby ring, the cause of so much heartache and loss of life, is still safely stored with Gran and Rose in my Susie Cooper teapot. Would he have come here looking for it next? Perhaps after he tried to dump me in the water he would have come and broken into Crumbs and searched through my belongings for it. The thought of that vile person breaking in and rummaging through my drawers and cupboards makes me feel sick.

Sally and the girls are working hard in Crumbs whilst I'm staying out of prying eyes in the kitchen for now. I just can't face all the well wishes and the rubberneckers again. How on earth do film stars cope? With what they earn I suppose it outweighs the inconvenience, no never!

Al and Nariman have heard about it on Radio Leeds. They are two of the few people I really want to talk to. Both of them are still shocked by the whole thing, starting with the murder in Café Miro and ending with Crumbs' involvement and my almost untimely watery death. Nariman says he is baking his wonderful bread today for lunch with them tomorrow. My favourite grilled halloumi, veg and salad sandwich in his fresh bread drizzled with his fantastic dressing, it's mouth-wateringly gorgeous.

So much is whizzing around my mind about all this it's almost unbelievable how I have been connected throughout with it all. When I have given my statement to Cameron, I'm hoping I will find out a bit more of the puzzle. Something has just jolted through my brain, where is Rose? She hasn't been through to tell me off or indeed say anything to me, that's not normal for her. I did try the thought transfer to thank her as I'm 99% sure it was her who appeared to Cameron warning him of my near drowning. Rose didn't even come and shock me whilst I was soaking in the bath, odd.

Ping, ping, my oven timer is singing away, rock buns and raspberry buns are ready for the cooling racks. Next is the pineapple upside down cake and a cherry crumble cake to make then I'm all done for the day.

Glancing at my wall clock I can see there's not much time to go and I have managed so far to keep well away from the curious customers.

"Hello Kate, sorry to sneak in the back way I couldn't face anybody." Pippa has arrived just before closing with a beautiful bouquet of flowers looking immaculate but with a very sad air about her. I should be buying flowers for my friend, she's grieving but in a different way, perhaps more for her late husband Humphrey all over again.

"Ooh, come in Pippa it's fine, I'm just a little jumpy and like you I'm keeping a low profile."

"I can't stay long I just wanted to see you and thank you for everything Kate. When this settles down will you come and have a meal with me, please?"

"Of course, I will. Are you sure you are alright Pippa?" I'm really concerned about her; this must be worse for Pippa than anyone else.

"It will take time Kate but as you know only too well. I have to keep in mind how it could have been, no hotel, no money, married to a bigamist and what's evident now, a murderer." She kissed me with tears welling up in her eyes.

"I'll call you tomorrow, Pippa, take care," I said hugging her hard.

Cameron came late looking tired with a young-looking detective constable in tow. My statement was taken in between coffee and bites of fresh rock buns all crunchy and fruity. Detective Constable Webster is in his element, a lovely young man. It's officially true, the police are looking younger each year.

Mr Potter has taken Flossie for her last evening walk; I don't know how I ever got such lovely people around me. Still no appearance from Rose but tomorrow is another day.

The sun is shining, the birds are singing I could almost pretend nothing has ever happened, except for my blackened eye. Last month my neck was all bruised, now my eye and cheek bone are plus scraped knees. Give it a couple of days and I will have a real shiner. If anyone asks, I'm going to say I'm a pole dancer and I fell awkwardly, that'll be a conversation stopper for sure.

After my lunch at Miro I've decided to do something I have put off for far too long. It's so easy to hide behind work instead of facing up to what should be done. Lawnswood cemetery is a short drive through Headingley, passing my happy childhood home and up towards Lawnswood, that's where I'm going with flowers and Flossie.

Walking through the front door to Café Miro I've been met by shouts, clapping and even customers taking photos of me. My friends Al and Nariman and a few regular customers have really made me blush. Heck! I'm no Miss Marple or Jessica Fletcher but they are treating me like a star, which to be honest isn't my kind of world. On the plus side my grilled halloumi, veg and salad sandwich is too good to be true, I'm savouring every mouthful. As usual Flossie has her own bowl with some sausages cut into bite size portions, they always spoil her.

"Here we are Kate your favourite, baked chocolate cheesecake and strawberries, baked especially for you," Nariman winks laughing loudly.

"Wow! Thank you just a small portion please." I'm so thrilled he thought of this.

"Since when did we do small portions? Give her a good slice Nariman with plenty of cream, she needs it!" Al jokes.

"Since even the smell of my baking puts extra calories on Al, look at these hips."

"I like my women curvy."

"You just like women Al," Nariman says throwing his hands up in the air. Al and Nariman are looking at each other. That look means they have something to say to me.

"Come on, come out with it you two!"

"We hate to ask you so soon after all that's happened, but we need to know as much as you think you are able to tell us," Al asks carefully.

"Yes, only if you can Kate. Enjoy your cheesecake first." Nariman looks serious.

In between sipping my flat white coffee I've told them everything from the day I came to Miro to the almost fatal event by the river. As yet I haven't been told of them finding a body washed up anywhere. The only part I've left out is my niggly doubts about him jumping into the water to escape. Nariman is looking at me with a puzzled expression on his face.

"There's just one thing I don't understand. You said he couldn't swim so why did he jump?"

You can't get much past these two, both are good businessmen with exceptionally clever minds.

"Exactly! All we know for sure is that he is a liar, big time. Perhaps he lied to Pippa about not being able to use her swimming pool. Don't forget Flossie then bit him, he went to hospital but lied and said it was a sports injury. Sports injuries don't come with teeth marks."

"That's right, it could be that," Al piped up from behind the counter.

Well, the more I think of my quick answer the more plausible it is. The trouble is if he can swim then he could still be alive somewhere. With all my heart I pray this is not possible. Thinking this makes me feel such a terrible person but for a lot of good peoples' sakes I need there to be a body found and soon!

It's a long time since I walked through these cemetery gates. Turning left and walking along the tree lined path at least I have Flossie with me who seems to be giving a doggy grin, wagging her tail and gently woofing at different trees with plaques. It's as though she is acknowledging the presence of those departed whose final resting places are alongside the path. This is entirely possible with my little pooch.

When I reach the large circle where each day's funeral flowers are laid out, I have to take the path to the left of it. Straight ahead of me is a grassy area with quite a few mature trees where loved ones' ashes have been carefully dug in around their roots. Plaques denote those loved ones resting there. A cherry tree was planted for Gran, and I thought it right to put her best friend, my lovely godmother Rose, with her, well except for the toes etc in my teapot!

The roses in my bouquet are all different shades of pink, the colour they both loved. Tears are already pricking my eyes, this place always does it to me no matter how beautiful and peaceful it is. Loss of a loved one leaves a big void in our lives. It's an ache which never goes away completely and to me it shows how much they were loved in life. Gran always said that our departed loved ones are only a thought away. Time has shown to me with the passing of Rose just how true that is. I don't think Gran meant it quite the way Rose does. Flossie is grinning, her tail wagging and she's running across the boggy grass ahead of me.

"Flossie, you don't know which tree, come back girl, wait for me."

Flossie knows. She is sitting at the base of the cherry tree looking up to the large branch to the right stretching out across the grass. Sitting side by side on the branch with their legs dangling over singing away are my Gran and Rose. This is the first time I have seen Gran and the second time I've seen Rose.

"We just called to say we love you. We just called to say how much we care. We just called to say we love you and we mean it from the bottom of our hearts." They're singing our favourite Stevie Wonder song we used to all sing and dance to in Gran's house, usually after they had drunk a few sherries. I'm trying my hardest to join in even though the tears are streaming down my face, nose running, voice croaking. This is the most special moment of all time. Standing on the boggy grass looking up at them I know I will always be protected and loved by them no matter how far away they may be. It is so true my wonderful loving Gran always said, "our loved ones are only a thought away."

How time flies but the memories remain. It's now three weeks later and the police have uncovered a lot to do with Slimeball. Thankfully they have managed to trace his wife's family for her burial. As yet he cannot be held accountable for all his crimes as no body has been found. Strange circumstances connected me with the murder and the situations in my home area. Perhaps it was a case of me being in the right place at the right time, otherwise the police would still be chasing the German. Somehow, I have a feeling Rose and Gran hold the answer to that! Life is precious but he destroyed so many, let us hope he doesn't have the opportunity to destroy any lives again.

# Books In This Series

*The Crumbs Mysteries*
1. Seeing is Believing
2. Murder at Café Miro
3. When the Tea Leaves Spell Murder

## Seeing Is Believing

After six weeks special leave of absence from work, Kate Philips' neat, orderly life is suddenly blown to smithereens. They say everything comes in threes and for Kate nursing her beloved Godmother through her last days was only the beginning. Returning home she finds not only has she been made redundant but her sports journalist husband has been getting his quarter pounders and dessert from a blonde bimbo with five stars from McDonalds. Resorting to cake and chocolate, the baking and eating of being her two cures for all, life takes another jolt with an unexpected inheritance.

Kate settles into her new life as owner of Crumbs tearooms in the pretty Yorkshire market town of

Wetherby. Hard work, reaching 30 and divorce don't faze her but her deceased Godmother Rose does. Inheriting and running the tearooms is one thing. Rose's sudden ghostly twitterings in Kate's ear and psychic interference leading to Kate's involvement in murder and mayhem is quite another.

## When The Tea Leaves Spell Murder

As Halloween approaches, Crumbs café is hosting an evening of clairvoyance for charity and it's a sell-out. Everybody is hoping for their loved ones to come through, but the last thing Kate wants is Rose, her ghostly godmother, to appear and wreak havoc. The event brings far more than just messages from loved ones when the clairvoyant is disturbed by what she sees.

In the weeks that follow, once again fear closes in on the residents of Wetherby as murders rock the town. Ignoring her godmother's advice, Kate's sleuthing leads her into dangerous territory as she tries to piece together the clues.

# Books By This Author

## Angels Can Be Hairy Too!: Flossie's First Case

A children's book featuring Flossie from The Crumbs Mysteries series.

Flossie may be small for a Jack Russell but she is no ordinary dog. She has just landed back on Earth for her first assignment as a Dog Angel with these instructions:

1. FOLLOW YOUR NOSE FLOSSIE

2. DON'T TRY TO FLY TOO SOON

3. REMEMBER THE ANIMAL ANGEL ACADEMY'S MOTTO: "ONLY FOR THE GOOD OF OTHERS"

She will try her best to follow them, whatever lies ahead. Join Flossie on her first adventure in England and see how she uses her special powers to solve the case.

## 292 Albion Place

When Nigel and Lorraine take on a new venture little do they realise just how much 292 Albion Place has in store for them. Launching two businesses within the same Victorian building on a street of trendy coffee shops in Leeds isn't so easy. Nigel struggles with his new café 'Hot Stuff!' on the floors below whereas upstairs 'Chic', Lorraine's hairdressing salon, prospers and she expands into beauty therapy. Their working days are far from mundane as 'Hot Stuff!' gets involved in a police stake out whilst 'Chic' salon is plagued by ghostly hauntings. Lorraine however is determined to let nothing stop her future plans. She has a colourful past accepted by Nigel and never spoken of. Secrets have a way of catching up with you, so does the past. Will the activities of a new member of staff threaten to put Lorraine's businesses and private life in jeopardy?

Printed by Amazon Italia Logistica S.r.l.
Torrazza Piemonte (TO), Italy